The Mysteries of

HUMMINGBIRD
FALLS

The Mysteries of

HUMMINGBIRD
FALLS

Joanne Clarey

Published by Alabaster Books
North Carolina

Published by Alabaster Books
P.O. Box 401
Kernersville, North Carolina 27285

Book design by
D.L.Shaffer
Cover Concept and design by
Joanne Clarey and David Shaffer

Second Edition

ISBN:09768108-1-6

Library of Congress Control
Number: 2005903770

ACKNOWLEDGEMENTS

Thank you to all the members of the Writers Roundtable: Dixie Land, Lynette Hall Hampton, David Shaffer, Kathryn Fisher, John Staples, Helen Goodman, and Larry Jakubsen for their encouragement and support.

Thanks to Alabaster Books and Dave Shaffer for the book design and publishing expertise.

Thank you to Anne Garland who loaned me her front porch and cheered me on.

Thank you to Brandon and Jessie Clarey who listened and critiqued with wisdom and graciousness.

To all the others along the way, thank you for your time, critique and care.

Chapter 1

AT TEN-THIRTY I heard a knock at the front door of my cottage. I had already locked the door and turned the lights out and was on my way to the bedroom, with my latest Down East Magazine, to settle in for a good read before sleep. The living room was pitch dark. I hadn't turned the motion lights on.

I hesitated. Living alone on a rural mountain road, I was apprehensive about opening the door to a late night caller, especially in this small town where most of the people I knew were in bed by now. Should I pretend I was already asleep and didn't hear the knock? Who would come calling at this time of night anyway?

The knock sounded again, not loud, more like a tap tapping. I quietly made my way to the door and peered out through the glass.

The long June days slowly gave way to a lingering twilight, so even at this late hour I could see someone silhouetted against the dark gray sky, standing on my porch, dripping from the drizzle that had been falling for hours. My visitor was wrapped head to toe in layers of clothes. The head was sheathed in a covering that appeared to be a beekeeper's hat and veil.

I called through the door. "Who is it? What do you want?"

"Shhh," the cloaked stranger whispered. "Be quiet. They might be watching, even now."

I knew then that my night visitor was Josie and I unlocked and opened the door and whispered, "Come in, Josie. What are you doing out tonight? You shouldn't be out in the dark all alone."

I pulled her in the door and shut it quickly before the bugs could sneak in. She rubbed where I had touched her and then blew on the spot.

"I'm sorry Josie, I forgot. I won't touch you again. I promise. Sit down. I'll just turn the lights on and get you something to drink. OK?"

"Don't turn the lights on, Ellie. They'll see. And I can only drink Dr. Pepper, you know. The rest have all been contaminated."

"OK, Josie. Then let's just sit down and you tell me what's going on."

"I'll stand if it's okay with you. That way my germs stay with me and I don't pick up yours off the material on the chairs. Plus, no fingerprints will be left here. That's important."

For a moment, I was frightened. Why would Josie want to avoid leaving fingerprints in my house? Did she have some insane plan in mind? I knew Josie had problems, mental health problems, to be specific, but I understood her to be harmless, at least to others.

Josie lived alone, several miles up the road from me, down a dirt road. She had been a well-known poet at one time, the story went, who lost her lover and then her reason. Now she was extremely paranoid, spinning tales of persecution, undercover agents and a host of other delusions that unfortunately dominated her life and led to involuntary stays at the State Hospital when she stopped taking care of herself. Several members of the Hummingbird Falls' Little Church's Community Health Committee visited Josie on a regular basis to check on her welfare. I saw Josie quite often as she would stop outside my porch at least once a week and chat with me about the latest conspiracy she was investigating or read me a poem from the scraps of paper she kept in the many pockets of the numerous layers of garments she wore. I always found her to be a rather sweet eccentric woman even though she was often lost in her own world.

"Tell me why you're here, Josie."

"I know who did it."

"Who did what, Josie?"

"Who killed Alice," she whispered.

"Alice?" I stammered. "Alice isn't dead."

"Oh, yes she is, Ellie. Alice is very, very dead."

"No, Josie. You must be mixed up. Alice is alive and well. I saw her only a few days ago."

"That may be, Ellie. But she's dead now. She was killed tonight and I saw it happen."

"Not Alice, she's my good friend, Josie. You must be mistaken. She couldn't be dead. Are you sure you saw someone being killed, Josie? What makes you think it was Alice?"

"I'm telling you, I saw Alice dead, killed, dead. How many times do I have to tell you? She is dead."

Josie was starting to wave her arms in the air and rock back and forth rather rapidly.

"If you're sure you saw something, Josie, then we'll have to call Dave, and the police will have to come to investigate. This is very serious. Are you positive you saw Alice being killed?"

"I just told you, didn't I? Of course, I saw it all. And I know who killed her too. But we can't call the police. They won't believe me; you know that. Even I know that. And then, if we did tell, the killer will know I saw what happened and will kill me. So, we can't tell the police. Promise me, promise you won't tell."

She repeated that phrase, over and over until I was yelling over and over that I wouldn't tell. I could see I was losing control of this situation, or perhaps I never had any control to begin with. But I wasn't sure what I could do to quiet Josie down.

By now Josie was nearing hysteria. The wrappings around her body had begun to shift and she tripped over the shawls and sweaters as they fell down her body and tangled with her feet. Her beekeeper's hat had fallen back, the net torn in a dozen places, revealing her wild white hair, very wrinkled pale face, clownishly colored with brightly rouged red cheeks, and wide-open terrified blue shadowed eyes.

She waved her hands around in the air like a windmill, saying, "Don't tell, don't tell. I never should have told you. I thought you were my friend and not one of them. I thought you would help me to catch that horrible person who hurt poor Alice. What a mistake. It was a mistake to trust you, to trust anyone. I never should have told you. What am I going to do?"

Then before I could say anything, Josie pulled a huge butcher knife out of the inner pocket of one of her many layers of clothes. She pointed it at me. She took a step closer to me and said, "I have this with me all the time, for protection, or to take care of things if they get too big. This is too big. You can't tell the police. They will get me. The killer will get me. I'm sorry I told you. Oh dear. You will have to be eliminated from the plan."

I just stood there in shock watching this crazy decrepit old woman waving a butcher knife at me, while her beekeeper's hat was falling off her head to the floor along with several layers of shabby, worn out garments. My mind was reeling with what to say or do. What did she mean by, "You will have to be eliminated"?

"Josie," I whispered. "Do you hear that?"

I instantly got her attention and distracted her from whatever plan she had been determined to carry out.

"What? What noise did you hear?" she asked.

I lied. "I thought I heard a car pull up. Mike was going to stop by to check on me tonight. Maybe he's here now. You don't want him to find you, do you? Why don't you sneak out the back door and slip down to your house? Then he won't ask you any questions. You can come by tomorrow and I'll try to help you."

"Good idea, good idea. I'll get gone for now. But we're not finished, Ellie. Don't go thinking that the crazy woman will forget, because I won't. I see a lot and I know a lot and I don't forget much. There are those who wish I would forget. That's part of my problem. I'll be back. But you better watch yourself because there's a murderer loose. And maybe you aren't safe either."

With that said, Josie pushed her bee keeper's hat and veil down over her head and scooped up her various garments from the floor and ran out the back door. I watched her quietly slip into the woods beside the cottage. I knew she would quickly become invisible because she had been traveling the trails through these woods for decades and knew each twist and turn. She could appear anywhere as if from nowhere anytime she wanted. She was wiser to the ways of nature, than she was of humans.

I shut the door, sorry that I had tricked her, taken advantage of her paranoia. But, I wasn't sure what she might do and I didn't want to take the chance. Now, I had to decide what to do about what had happened. One thing Josie said was true. No one would believe her story. I didn't believe it myself. If I did call the police, they would probably just brush it off as another of her insane delusions. But what if she did see something? What if Alice or someone had been killed tonight? Josie could be holding valuable information if there had been a murder. I felt I had to call the police, just in case.

But first I would do some checking of my own. I picked up the phone and dialed Alice's number. At least I could find out if she was OK. It had only been a couple of days since I had seen her. Perhaps it was closer to a week. I knew her brother was coming to town and that she was nervous about his visit. They hadn't seen each other for thirteen years. Their relationship had been a troubled one. I had decided to give them space for themselves and had cancelled our regular dinner meeting, telling Alice to call if she wanted to get together. But, she hadn't called. Come to think of it, I hadn't seen Alice or talked to her since her brother arrived. The phone rang and rang. Finally, the answering machine came on with Alice's voice requesting that I leave a message after the tone.

"Alice, are you there?" I asked. I waited. Then I said, "Alice, call me when you get this message. It's very important. I don't care what time it is. Just call me. It's Ellie."

Now I was in a dilemma. I didn't know whether Alice was all right, but I didn't have any reason to believe that Alice wasn't all right, other than what Josie told me. If what Josie had told me was true, and I revealed her story to the police, I could endanger Josie with the unknown murderer, or perhaps even cause suspicion that she knew about the murder because perhaps she had committed it herself. On the other hand, if I said nothing, the killer might get away, whether it was Josie or someone else, and I would be shirking my duty as a citizen. Of course, the whole story was probably the creation of the mad poet, in which case I would be seen as a fool for reporting Josie's delusion. But I was worried because I couldn't reach Alice.

Just as I was reaching for the phone to call Dave Shaffer, Chief of the Hummingbird Falls Police, it rang, startling me.

"Yes," I said. "Alice, is it you?"

"Hi there, Ellie. Not Alice, sorry. It's Colby Conners here. Sorry to call so late, but I am just checking on you, lovely lady, to make sure everything is all right up there in the mountains. This rain keeps the roads pretty slippery. How are you doing up there all by yourself?"

Colby Conners, a young, handsome cop, served under Dave as the only other police officer in town. I knew him by sight, but he had never called to check up on me before, no matter what the weather. I thought it strange that he would call me now and so late.

"It is really late, Colby, but thanks for your concern. Yes, I'm fine. But maybe I should tell you about..."

He interrupted me before I could finish my sentence. "Don't want to bother you or keep you from what you were doing, Ellie, which I am sure was pretty interesting, knowing you, but I was wondering if you saw Josie today. I stopped by her place several times and she doesn't answer the door. Not that I expected her to answer, you know. She doesn't like the police, men, or anyone who comes to her door. But I wanted to make sure she was all right, just the same. Have you seen her?"

For some reason unknown to me, I answered, "No, Colby. I didn't see her today." This was not an actual lie I assured myself, because I didn't see her in the day, only tonight, which technically wasn't day. I was curious about the coincidence of Josie's bizarre story and Colby's inquiries about her.

"Are you calling everyone up here tonight? Has something happened that I should know about?"

He hesitated. "No M'ame. Nothing unusual has occurred that I'm aware of. I'm just checking out the beautiful women who live up the hill." He laughed. "Got to keep up that reputation of mine. No, seriously, I don't have enough time for calling everyone. But you and Josie both being alone up so far, I just thought I'd put a little extra effort in. Are you sure you didn't see her? She sometimes comes down to visit you, I heard. Some say she confides in you more than she does most, you being so nice and all."

I was beginning to be irritated by Colby's sugary sweet talk. He appeared to be trying to flatter me into revealing something he wanted to hear. Why was he so interested in Josie, a harmless crazy old lady?

"No, I told you before, Colby. I didn't see her today. Why do you keep asking about Josie? Are you especially worried about her?"

"Actually, I am. The Little Church ladies called us today and said Josie was acting strangely and may not be taking her meds. She just returned from the State Hospital last week. So I am trying to follow up on her."

"The only thing I can tell you is that the last time I did see Josie, she wasn't suicidal. I'm pretty sure of that. But she was acting a little weird."

"Well, I'll drop by her place again and see if I can locate her."

"Could you let me know if she's okay, if you do talk with her? Maybe I could be of some help to her if she needs it."

"Sure, be glad to. Give me a chance to chat with you again. I'd enjoy that. So I'll notify you. Don't worry. Now lock up good. Sleep well. I'll take care of things. Goodbye."

I hung up the phone, disturbed. Why hadn't I told him about Josie? And why was he so determined to find her that he would call me so late at night?

I locked the back and front doors and checked the windows, too. A big four-wheel drive truck passed slowly by, the spotlights on top lighting up the sides of the road. Probably illegal night hunters jacking deer. As they passed, I saw the rifle rack was filled. I hope they weren't taking themselves too seriously. And I hoped that Josie was deep in the woods on her way home, out of spotlight range. I remembered to put the motion lights on and trudged off to bed, worrying about Alice, Josie, Colby and what I should do about the situation I found myself in. I always seem to get myself into some thing or another, even though I try so hard to just mind my own business. I bet I wouldn't get much sleep tonight.

Chapter 2

FOG ERASED THE mountains one by one, first Rattlesnake Mountain, then Hurricane and finally Owl's Head Mountain. It eclipsed the foothills and sank down into the valley covering Hummingbird Falls Township. White mist rose from the falls into the forest and then crept out, smothering the field across Durkin Farm Road. Stealthily it skulked its way to the screen porch where I was drinking my second cup of morning coffee. I heard the robins calling and the lonely crow cawing from the dead tree at the edge of the lawn, but other than a far away buzz of an early morning chain saw, the forest around the cottage I had rented for the last ten summers was as still as the hush before the breaking of a massive thunderstorm and invisible as a ghost at dawn. Even the crimson red hummingbird feeder at the edge of the open porch was muted and no hover of wings interrupted my thoughts.

I have been coming to Hummingbird Falls every summer since the death of my husband, Christopher, ten years ago. My two children and I needed a change of scenery and a quiet place to pull ourselves together. The years before Chris died from prostate cancer had been filled with hospitals, hospice and overwhelming fear and sadness. After his death we were lost. The tiny village of Hummingbird Falls, surrounded by protective mountains and national forest lands was a healing place. I could rest up from my year of teaching English to mostly reluctant city kids and distract myself from my loss with gardening and writing. Sandy and Allison found summer jobs and new friends at the inns and golf courses that attracted tourists from around the world. As the children grew older and became busy with friends, then college, journeys and other activities that didn't require a mother's attendance, I traveled to

Hummingbird Falls by myself. Now Sandy is married and settled in Florida and Allison pursues her marketing career in Ohio. They welcome my two or three visits a year with love, and will sometimes spend a week or more up here in the cottage with me. I know their lives are full and I have become a loving chapter in their biographies, no longer the protagonist of their stories, except, of course, when they run into the crises that plaque all young adults. Then I become their dependable mom once again, until the crisis passes away. Thankfully, right now Sandy and Allison were both experiencing good times.

I have learned to enjoy my time alone, although loneliness is a visitor I entertain too often. After Chris died, I first grieved, then accepted and finally became content to live life on my own. Teaching keeps me busy for most of the year and I love the challenge of the classroom and adolescents. Most often, I relish the independence that is now mine. But I also adore quiet and solitude, and my love of nature flourishes in these mountains. So I return here each summer and now, ten years later, I find myself completely in love with Hummingbird Falls. My creativity has been unleashed. I paint with oils, covering canvases with beautiful mountains, rivers, fields, and antique houses when I wish. And I write my poetry and essays on the little screen porch. I garden and love the feel of digging into the rich dark earth. I find the small town life of Hummingbird Falls perfect for me from June to September.

When I drive from the suburbs each June, and finally arrive at the covered bridge that leads into Hummingbird Falls, I am greeted by a vision of the past. Historical capes and Victorian homes encircle the town green. The village streets are clean, filled with little shops and small eateries. Flowerbeds are bright with perennials and annuals and grass is neatly cut. No Golden arches, neon signs or chain stores blemish the landscape.

Each day my mail is handed to me with a smile in the tiny post office run by Sarah Moody and at the town offices no question goes unanswered by Bonnie Leonard and Debby Jackson, the administrative assistants to the selectmen of the town. They know everything that is going on in town and don't mind sharing it, in confidence, of course.

On the ground floor of the town hall, Dave Shaffer and Colby Conners man the Police Department.

Along with Heppie's Flower Shop, Reggie's Deli, Margaret Joyner's Art Gallery, and several gift, antique and curio shops and small restaurants lining the main street, the town library, The Little Church, and The Inn by the Bridge face the stone bridge at the bottom of Hummingbird Falls, one of the village's major tourist attractions. The bigger, more luxurious Inns and tourist lodges are situated up the mountain roads, closer to the skiing areas, the incredible mountain views, the many hiking trails and the beautiful mountain rivers which cascade down, and then come together, forming the Coldwater River which feeds the famous Hummingbird Falls.

Hummingbird Falls was named after the flock of Ruby Throated Hummingbirds that arrive each spring and take up residence on the edges of the falls, where wild flowers grow abundantly. The birds nest in the trees near the water, raise their young, and whirl over the rapids in colorful iridescent displays that delight everyone who visits. Eventually, the residents of the village, which had been called Washington, Adams, then Madison, renamed the township after the falls. The township of Hummingbird Falls pays tribute not to a passing president, but to the unique beauty that lies within its own town borders.

The Hummingbird Falls are spectacular and bring thousands of tourists to the site each year. Water tumbles down the Coldwater River from the range of mountains that encircle the northern side of the valley that holds the town of Hummingbird Falls. As the river descends, it rips and roars around curves, through rocky chasms, and under numerous bridges. Finally, about 500 feet above the town of Hummingbird Falls the river begins its finale with a flashing fury of water over rocks, beginning with three cascades. These three rocky staircases, each of them about twelve feet high, splash the river onto huge boulders that split the flow of water in two individual set of rapids. Then the river joins again and glides at an angle of forty five degrees about fifty feet down under the Iron Bridge and into the first of many deep pools that dot the falls and make them famous for their cold water swimming. Then small waterfalls join the rapid current that pulls the water through a series of rough boulders topped with moss which cut the silver slips of water as they brawl on down to a narrower section, overhung with beech trees. From there the river widens again and water pours down over smoothed river rocks, granite boulders and jagged stones, collecting several more times into deep dark swimming holes, before it hurtles on to the last major cascade, a plunge of thirty-five feet down a rocky staircase. There the river slows as it reaches the valley floor and the village. It runs over smaller rocks with a babble and a splash and then under the town's lower stone bridge. The river continues its journey through the notch and on down to the even larger rivers that eventually lead to the sea.

When the current is slower, and I am brave enough to enter the ice cold water, I can swim or walk to the middle of falls and see an incredible view of Moby Mountain which rises to the south of Hummingbird Falls. When I look down into the clear clean water, I can see the bottom covered with stones of all shapes and color. The mica covered rocks glint in the sunlight like gold. Mother Nature was at her best when she created Hummingbird Falls. Its beauty takes my breath away every time I see it.

This morning, the weather was too foggy and drizzly to swim, hike, paint, garden, or write on the screen porch. I tried to reach Alice again, but only got her answering machine. I left another message. Josie's tale from last night was bothering me, even though I still doubted its veracity, and I needed to be sure that Alice was all right. I decided I would drive into town, stop by Alice's home and talk with her and reassure myself. Then I would pick up my mail, go to the laundromat, and check out new arrivals in the tiny Hummingbird Falls Library, which nestles between the Little Church and the river at the bottom of the falls. Maybe I would stop in the pastry shop for one of their specialties, blueberry turnovers. Those blueberry turnovers have added more than a few pounds to my already plump body. But I don't let that stop me. Eating sweets is one of the last vices I have going for me.

The fog was so thick I had to use my wipers as well as my lights as I slowly drove down Durkin Farm Road toward town. I decided to turn on to the Falls Road, as I often do, to see the Coldwater River, tucked into a narrow fold between rapidly rising peaks. The road follows the river which drains the snow-capped hills during the spring melt off and collects the heavy rains that fall during June. We had endured days of pouring rain in the last two weeks and I knew the water coursing down the five hundred foot drop of rapids, pools and falls would be wild and fun to watch.

The roads around the township of Hummingbird Falls are mountain roads, windy and treacherous. They need constant care to keep potholes and frost heaves in check and shoulders reinforced after heavy rains. The Hummingbird Falls' town road crew, headed up by Larry Jacobs, literally knows each and every twist, turn, rise and fall in Hummingbird Falls' thirty five miles of roadways. One of their daily and most important duties is to monitor Hummingbird Falls. The Falls are what bring the tourists and the money to Hummingbird Falls Township. They check for blockages, high water, contamination, and proper access to the water from the parking area along the Falls Road. They empty trash and pick up litter along both sides of the falls.

This week Larry, the road crew chief, had stopped by the cottage to tell me we were in for a lot more rain, thunderstorms and damp, dark days. The long-term weather forecast reported that we were stuck in the middle of a rain producing weather pattern that could continue for weeks. Larry added that many of the early hurricanes this year were dumping heavy rain when they hit the mountains. Just a few days ago, eight inches of rain had fallen in twenty-four hours. Although the tail end of the hurricanes rarely brought heavy winds to the mountains, they could bring record-breaking amounts of rain. Several more tropical storms were all ready approaching the southeast coast. If they veered inland with more record rainfalls, the water table would be overflowing and with it, the rivers, streams, brooks, creeks, ponds, and ditches. He was warning all the townsfolk about the deteriorating condition of the roads, due to higher than usual run off from the mountains that encircled Hummingbird Falls. Several culverts had already caved in, causing washouts. The gravel and dirt shoulders were eroding as fast as the crew could ditch them open. The area had experienced a record spring rainfall and June had already produced a new record for the meteorologist's history books.

Before I arrived at the turn off Durkin Farm Road to the Iron Bridge that crosses the upper falls, I saw red lights flashing through the mist. A sawhorse formed a roadblock and I had to pull to a stop behind three other cars and a green Hummingbird Falls' maintenance truck. The occupants of the other vehicles had left their cars and I put my hazard lights on and did the same, making my way forward to where a small crowd clustered around an ambulance and the Chief of Police's big black SUV. Flashlights were winking through the thick fog like fireflies and the SUV's flashing blue and red lights illuminated a yellow and black crime scene tape stretched across the road ahead.

"What happened ?" I asked. I realized that the roar of the falls was so loud that no one could hear me. I yelled, "Hey, what happened?"

"Can't rightly say, Ellie," yelled back the Chief, David Shaffer. "Bobby Brady, summer hire for the maintenance crew, was checking around the falls this morning, just as he usually does. And Larry had told him to be on the look out for trees, branches or rocks that might have been loosened by the increased water flow and causing trouble, blockage or what not, so he was looking good. Said he had to go right up to the edge to even see half way across in this fog. He spotted what he thought was a bundle of clothes hung up on a rock down near the bottom of the falls, before the lower bridge. Bobby put the hook out there and caught the mess and was hauling it in when he noticed the clothes contained a body. Freaked him out good. And no wonder. The body is pretty battered and broken up. The face is unrecognizable. Pretty tough thing for a young man to see. He radioed Larry and Larry called me and Colby. We fished it out and called the State Police. They have been on the scene for a while, examining the body and working their way up the falls, looking for anything unusual. We think she went off this bridge, so we have to close it to gather any evidence that may be here. You folks have to back up, turn around and take the Notch Road to town."

"Do you know who it is?" asked Mike Greeley, whose teal Subaru was parked in front of my red Subaru. Subaru's are the car of choice around here because of their four-wheel drive and cold weather start up consistency. Mike's family has lived here for at least six generations and he is the last of his line. He still hays the big fields on the side of Little Diamond Mountain further up the road from the cottage where I was staying, even though he doesn't make enough money from the hay to justify the gas to run the big John Deere. Every once in a while he will sell a piece of his acreage to pay his overdue bills. The condominiums that sprang up in place of the forest-lined fields upset the local townspeople. Hummingbird Falls' long time residents want everything to stay just the way it used to be years ago. So Mike is alienated from many of the people he has known all his life, and he distances himself, attending town meetings, hanging in the pastry shop, but little else. Right now he is living alone on the big farm, and stops by to chat with me when he sees me on the porch. I think he can talk to me because I am not one of the long time local people. I enjoy his company and he seems to enjoy mine. I have cooked dinner for him several times and he has taken me fishing at his favorite secret place. We are amused by many of the same things, we hate politics, and both know how to be still while the sun sets and the first stars pop out in the sky. His tall thin frame, sun wrinkled face and salt and pepper hair suggest an older and weaker man than he is. I have seen him lift bales of hay with one hand and throw them overhead onto a wagon. He is as fit as an Olympian athlete.

"I can't say anything about that, Mike, until the Medical Examiner and the State Police finish their work here, identify the body and talk to the relatives. It will all come out in a few days, I expect. Now just let me jot down your names, addresses and phone numbers for the record. You, too, Sam and Herbert. I have to note anybody who comes to the scene. Not that you are suspects, or anything. We don't even know what has happened here. When I'm done you can all turn around and go about your business. It is enough that those tourists will be swarming around as soon as the sun breaks up this fog, wanting to go swimming, picnicking, rock hunting and viewing Moby Mountain from the center of the falls. Then we are going to have a hell of a mess with cars trying to go every which way when they learn they just have to turn around and head back to town. I just bet I'll have complaints from here to Sunday."

I knew the Police Department was use to handling situations rather than crimes, as in many small towns. Chief David Shaffer grew up in Hummingbird Falls. His father, Walter, a former selectman, instilled a sense of civic duty in his son. He encouraged Dave to join the county Sheriff's office and after a short while Dave came home to Hummingbird Falls to work under Chief Lonny Skinner. Twelve years later he became the Chief himself. David told me that most people don't want to be chief in the town where they grew up. You have to deal with friends you went to school with, or older people who remember you as a kid playing ball in the schoolyard. The advantage is that you are on a first name basis and know people's personal history and situations.

Occasional domestic disputes, motor vehicle accidents, moose vs. car calls, weather related issues, irate or disruptive tourists and intoxicated drivers are the usual calls in Hummingbird Falls. Of course, the tourists crowding the little town require Dave and his good looking patrolman, Colby Conners, to be on call 24 hours a day. When they work their shift they take care of whatever comes up and the job requirements change from moment to moment. Today the job was to secure a body and determine who it was and whether the woman had committed suicide, had an accidental fall or was the victim of foul play.

While Dave was writing down names, I turned away and looked up the falls as far as I could see in the rain and fog, wondering if a murderer might be lurking there, hiding behind the firs, shrouded in the fog. The triple cascades were barely visible. I couldn't see very far down the falls either, not nearly as far as where the body must have ended up after it scraped, bounced, bumped and dropped three hundred and fifty feet. I could only imagine the damage done to the body of the poor soul who had been found dead today.

I joined the others and walked back to my car.

"What a terrible thing!" Mike said. "I wonder who it is. I can't believe someone died in the falls. This is awful."

"Has anyone every drowned in the falls before?" I asked.

"Never. There have been a few near misses, but I never heard of anyone who has ever died on the falls before. A few people have been injured when they lost their footing on the rocks and tumbled into the current and hit some rocks. A couple of drunken teens got hurt pretty badly when they decided to tube down the falls. And, years ago, way back when the first settlers came, a bad flood washed through the town. I think a couple of families were drowned when the river crested and swept their cabins away. But I never heard of anyone drowning or being killed in the falls. But meet me down at the pastry shop, Ellie. That place with be buzzing today and maybe someone there will remember better than me what all has happened at the falls."

Now I was certain that after I saw Alice I would go to the pasty shop, hangout for the local folks. The tourists drank their lattés and ate their goodies down at the new Starbucks on Rt. 43. But the pastry shop catered to residents. I guessed everyone who was anyone in the town would stop in there today to catch the gossip about the woman in the falls, to create theories about what happened and retell the legends and tales of disaster that accompanied the settling and growth of this small mountain town. My curiosity had been aroused and I, too, wanted to know what had happened, to whom and by whom. The mystery of Hummingbird Falls had gripped me and I suspected that my quiet solitude might have to be put aside until the mystery was solved.

"I'm just going to stop over to see Alice for a few moments and then I'll see you at the pastry shop, Mike. Good idea. Someone is bound to know the whole history of the falls. See you later."

Chapter 3

I DROVE UP Alice's long sugar maple tree lined drive to her impressive cedar shake three storied home. The house had a commanding view of the mountain ranges and on a clear day one could see the auto road that led to the top of the highest peak. The house was surrounded by well tended flower gardens, a variety of shrubbery and handsome century old trees, both hard wood, fir and pine. For a large house, it was surprisingly welcoming, with its wide front steps leading up to a porch that encircled the first floor. Antique rockers with caned seats lined the porch. Hanging baskets full of brilliant lobelias, petunias, geraniums, impatients and hanging ivy loaded the air with perfume. I spotted a hummingbird hovering around one of the baskets.

I knocked at the door and rang the bell. Alice's car was in the driveway so I was surprised when no one answered. Perhaps she had gone out with her brother. I didn't see any other car and I know he had driven up last week. I scribbled a quick message asking Alice to call me on the back of an old envelope I found stuffed in my purse and put it through the brass mail slot. I was sure I would catch up with her later today. As I walked back to my car, I turned around for another glance at Alice's beautiful home. So gracious a building and such a peaceful spot couldn't be the site of anything but goodness and happiness. Nothing evil would find its way here, I decided.

The pastry shop parking lot was full with old Volvos, four wheel drive pickup trucks, and other Subaru's, plus a few beat up Chevies and Fords. I had to park down by Margaret Joyer's Art gallery because the lot was so crowded. Inside, every booth was full and the clamor of voices roared almost as loud as the falls. When Elizabeth, the owner of the pastry shop, saw me come in, she yelled out to the crowd in a voice far bigger than her five foot two, one hundred pound body should have been capable of.

"Now, I'll say it again. You who have been in here longer than a half an hour, cozy up with some else and let the ones just coming in have some room. If we squeeze in tight everyone will have a seat."

The crowd laughed and someone yelled out, "I'll take Ellie at my table anytime." That produced more laughs and a series of invitations for various people to join others. Soon a version of musical chairs ensued, leaving some spaces available for those still in line at the counter.

When it was my turn, Elizabeth said, "What will you have, honey? We are low on everything, but Tom came in to help and more turnovers and cookies are just about ready to come out of the oven. Here, try the apple pie. I'll put a piece of cheese on it for you and then when the blueberry turnovers come out, I'll save one for you. You're white, no sugar, right?"

"That's right Elizabeth. You must be having a wild morning. How are you holding up?"

"Doing fine. I like it busy and I get to hear all the latest when someone new comes in. What do you know about it?"

"Well, I just came down from the upper bridge."

"Hold it." Elizabeth ordered. Then she hollered, "Folks, here is the latest report from the top of the falls. Go ahead, Ellie."

I could feel the blush move up my cheeks, but I turned around and faced the hushed and expectant audience. "Well, I don't really know anything at all."

The crowd groaned and looked so disappointed that I added, "But I just came down from the Iron Bridge and saw Dave, the ambulance crew and one of Larry's maintenance trucks. They have the road and the bridge blocked off and don't know how long it will be closed or how long the investigation will take. They won't say who it is, I mean, was, but did say it was a woman's body that was found at the bottom of the falls. They think she might have been thrown off the upper bridge or she jumped or maybe slipped. That's really all I know, except that the State Police are covering all the ground from where the body was found on up the falls to the bridge. That's it, I guess. Sorry I don't know more, but Dave said he couldn't say anything until the State Police released the official information."

"Mike already told us all that, Ellie. Don't you know anything new?" Reggie called out.

"Sorry," I said and looked for Mike. He was sitting in a booth full of men. He smiled at me and mouthed the word, sorry, to me.

The crowd turned back to one another and the buzz of talk filled the room again. Relieved that I was off the spot, I picked up my coffee and pie and stood looking for a place to sit.

"Over here, Ellie. We have room for you." called the town librarian, Pauline Hayes. She was sitting with Bonnie from the town office and Margaret who owned the art gallery.

"Thanks, I was afraid I would have to eat standing up."

"You wouldn't be the first today," said Margaret, stunning in a multicolored ankle length silk dress, as she made room for Ellie. She brushed back her glossy black hair from her carefully made up face.

Margaret continued, "Everyone's been in. Isn't it terrible? Nothing like this has happened in Hummingbird Falls since the Wilson family's murder back in 1991. They never did find the crazy person who taped up Mr. And Mrs. Wilson and then shot them to death."

"Remember, all they ever found of the daughter was her skull?" Bonnie added. "Wasn't that just too much? How grotesque. I wonder if that murderer came back. Oh, probably not, different MO. I learned about that on Forensic Files."

Pauline added quickly, "I was only a teenager then, still in high school. Callie Wilson was one of my friends. She was such a nice girl. Her parents were really strict and hardly let her do anything. So, I used to hang out at her house a lot."

"Really?" Asked Ellie. "That must have been hard for you."

"It was. But that night I was out with Colby. We only found out what happened when we went to school the next day. School was closed for three days and the funeral was so sad. It's weird to drive by that house now.

"Her uncle lives there with his family now," Bonnie said. "I wouldn't ever go in that house again after what happened, not if you paid me a million dollars. Nothing like that had ever happened before in Hummingbird Falls. And nothing like it has happened since, thank heavens."

Pauline said, "We were all so upset and scared. We were afraid to go out of our houses. It was grisly. Imagine, all they found was her skull. Where's the rest of her? At the time, we all looked at each other wondering if one of us was the killer."

Pauline's pretty face seemed to become paler. Her honey blonde hair fell into her eyes and she pushed the hair back revealing turquoise eyes and thick lashes. Her naturally pink lips pouted sensuously, even though she was talking about something that bothered her. She looked nervously around as if she were still trying to figure out which of us murdered the Wilsons.

Margaret continued, "I wonder sometimes if that killer is still around here. I get the creeps when I think of such a bad thing happening in our little town. And now some woman is found dead in the falls. I don't think anyone has ever died in the falls. I hope this poor soul just had an accident, plain and simple."

"I hope Dave has better luck this time," Bonnie said. "He had such a tough time with the Wilson investigation. Perhaps this incident will prove how much we need to expand some of our services. Only two police officers, for goodness sake."

Margaret said, "I been saying that for years. If we just let more businesses into this town and changed a few of those antiquated zoning restrictions, the tax revenue would pay for increasing services around here. Then maybe we could have our garbage picked up instead of having to go to the dump and have more police officers on the job, and maybe even a paid firefighter, instead of having to rely strictly on volunteers. New homes and new businesses would help us all financially."

Bonnie said, "Margaret, calm down. You are a group of one when it comes to believing that making changes to Hummingbird Falls would improve things. We do just fine the way we are. We don't want big business and condo developments here. We would just end up having to build new roads and new schools and then everything would go haywire. Let's not go over that issue all again."

"That fight you had in here last week with Alice when you advocated forming a group to invest in a MacDonald's franchise for the center of town should have let you know that she and most of the town are opposed to that kind of growth and change, said Pualine. "Now you've expressed your opinion; let's get back to the point."

Bonnie turned to the rest of us. Her pretty face was animated with curiosity, her brown eyes wide and her mouth open as she licked her lips, totally engaged in the most exciting mysteries to come her way in thirteen years.

"Who do you think the woman was? What do the rest of you think happened? Debbie and I were talking and we think she might be one of the group of women who are staying up in the Inn on Osprey Hill. Maybe she got lost in the fog and slipped in the river and got carried down by the current." Bonnie looked around the table for affirmation.

"Or," added Bonnie, as she warmed to the discussion, "she could be from anywhere and just decided Hummingbird Falls was where and drowning the way she wanted to die, dramatically and to make a big splash, so to speak. Oh, excuse me, I didn't mean it to sound funny. I feel bad, now. Someone dying is terrible. I just meant maybe she wanted some kind of attention, you know, not just to die regularly."

Reggie, the deli owner from down the street, leaned over from his booth into ours. "No, I don't think you are right. I think she might be one of us. Colby is checking on every family to see if someone is missing. You know some of those farms up hill are pretty secluded. Someone could be missing for a while and we'd never know it until Sunday at the Little Church when they didn't show up. That is, if they go to church."

"That's a good job for Colby," John Jenkins laughed from two booths down. "He likes visiting all the ladies around town so he'd be sure to know if one went missing."

The crowd snickered. We all knew about Colby's visits to various ladies. But who could resist his rugged good looks, muscled body and sky blue eyes? And it wasn't just his looks, either. He was utterly charming with his good manners and flattering country flirting style.

"Stop that right now, John," said Pauline. "You are just jealous. Colby is a fine hard working man. He is just friendly, that's all. I wish more were like him." I noticed she blushed as she scolded John.

"Well, what about that artist colony up White's Hill? Anything could be going on up there and nobody would ever know," added Reggie.

"Now, don't you discriminate against the artists, Reggie," answered Margaret. She turned and faced him, tossing her black hair with a fashionable flair. "Most of those folks are real nice and normal. I talk to them all the time at the gallery. They'd no more go murdering or suiciding than you or me. They just have artistic ways of thinking, dressing and communicating. They add color to the Saturday Farmers and Crafts Market and bring tourists in, too."

Mike shouted down from his booth, "If you ask me, it is one of those tourists who come here to reconcile their broken down marriage after it's already too rotten to save. They drink all night in the Jack Frost bar, end up drunk, yelling and fighting. Maybe one fight went too far and the husband threw his wife over the bridge."

The theories were flying as thick as black flies in the morning. Someone called out, "Have you seen Hattie, lately?"

"I saw her this morning at the post office."

"What about Alice, have you seen her?" someone else called out.

"Her brother is visiting. She's probably got her hands full with him."

The mention of Alice's name sent shivers down my spine. Josie's wild disclosures last night about seeing Alice murdered leaped into my mind.

Mumbling voices whispered across booths. A voice from the booth closest to the door said, "Then someone better check on her. That brother of her's is no good, never has been. Coming back here after thirteen years. What's that about?"

"Oh stop it, Frank. You don't know anything about Alice and her brother. Maybe they are just having a reunion," said Bonnie, managing a smile that made her dimple show. "He seems nice enough. He stopped in to look up the tax maps on Alice's place and was real pleasant to me."

Bonnie was the beauty of the town. Her dark brown hair shone under the pastry shop's lights and her pretty young face was clear with a peaches and cream complexion. But her light patter about Alice's brother didn't dispel my anxiety about what Frank had said about Alice's brother. I was even more worried now about Alice then before.

Another voice called out, "Then how about Josie?"

"I think she had to go back to the hospital again. Yes, she went in last week."

"Well, is she back? Someone certainly ought to check on her."

More names were thrown into the air. Most were accounted for, but dozens were possibilities that made the pastry sweet air turn sour. A gloom like the fog descended onto the crowd and we all finally quieted. Only an occasional hushed conversation could be heard, except for the back booth where an argument had arisen over who could be the murderer, if there was a murder. We could hear people talking outside the pastry shop now. They, too, seemed obsessed with identifying the dead woman and figuring out what happened to her.

By now I had finished my coffee, pie and the blueberry turnover that Elizabeth brought over. "I have to go do my errands, but if someone hears something will you give me a call, or leave a message on my answering machine? It is pretty creepy thinking that there could be a murderer running around, especially since I am up there all alone. I hope it wasn't a murder. An accident is bad enough."

Bonnie said, "I'll call you or I'll have Debbie call. We should be one of the first to hear the official word, that is, after Dave and Colby. We will let you know. Until then, lock your door and leave your motion lights on."

"I hate those motion lights," I answered. Every time they go on, I get nervous and then find out it is only a deer or a raccoon in the yard. But that is a good idea, Bonnie, thanks."

As I got up to leave, Mike called out, "Take care, Ellie. Until this is cleared up, there is a bunch of us who will be patrolling the roads, just in case. We will be driving by your cottage three or four times tonight, so don't be worried if you hear a slow moving car. And lock up tight. Maybe you should think about adopting a dog from the pound."

"Thanks guys," I answered as I made my way past the full booths and headed for the door. "I don't know about the dog. I love dogs, but I haven't been quite ready to get a new one after my lab Walter died several years back. But I'll think about it and I'll look out for your lights. If mine are on, stop in and get some coffee and a snack."

Living in a small town did give me a sense of security. At first, the townspeople were a bit cautious with me, wondering if I was just another tourist, or rich summer visitor. But after I returned to the same small cottage year after year, they learned I wasn't just a tourist, and they moved me to the category of a regular seasonal. As I reached out to make some new friends, they gradually came to accept me. When I started to look for land or a house to purchase so that I could move here year round when I retired, they began to treat me almost as if I were one of their own and that gives me a good feeling. I meet with Alice and Margaret often for dinner and make sure to stop and shop in all the local stores and chat with the owners. I am friendly with most all of the local folks who work here year round. I'm in the Post Office everyday to get my mail and talk with Sarah. If I went missing, someone would notice and look for me. Of course, it would probably be too late, like it was for the woman at the bottom of the falls, but at least I wouldn't end up bear food or turkey vulture dinner. I shivered this thought away and completed my errands and then headed for home. I watched the woods as I drove, looking for murderers, strangers, or suspicious people. I knew I wasn't as easy with my solitude now as I had been earlier this morning. I began to wish I had a dog, a big dog, a big dog whose bark would frighten away all intruders.

Chapter 4

I WOKE WITH a start at 5:15. I grabbed my glasses from the bedside table, got up and looked around the cottage. Everything appeared to be just as I had left it when I went to sleep. The door was locked, windows shut, motion light on. I shook my head. All this madness of a missing woman was spooking me. Usually, I am a pretty calm person, not given to fits, hysteria or wild thoughts. But, something about this bizarre situation had me churned up.

The drizzle had turned to rain during the night. Today would be another gloomy, clammy day. I would just have to try to ignore the weather or I would end up with cabin fever, depressed and moldy. I decided to try to settle down, get into my usual routine and be in the moment, as they say. So, I dressed, put on my walking shoes and my rain gear and headed out for my morning walk.

Everyone in the mountains bikes, walks, hikes the hills or jogs. Tourists and locals alike. Usually the tourists run so fast they forget to look around them. Most of the rest of us walk. It's great exercise, trudging up and down the hilly roads and the best way to get a view of the mountains, the little brooks that feed the Coldwater and Wildcat Rivers, and the wild creatures. 5:30 was a bit early for me, but I set out anyway.

I decided to walk up past Josie's road, just out of curiosity. I was moving along at a good clip when I heard a car coming up behind me going very fast. I stepped off the road onto the muddy shoulder as a Hummingbird Police black SUV came whizzing by. Its lights weren't blinking, and the siren was silent. What had happened now?

Fifteen minutes later I came to Josie's dirt road. There were deep tracks in the wet dirt of the road. Josie didn't have a car, so I knew someone had visited her recently. I peered down the road as far as I could see, but her house was around the bend and the trees blocked my view. I thought I might walk down to see her, to check on her, but decided not to. I didn't want to get into her story any deeper than I had to. If she decided to pursue it with me, then I would deal with it, but I didn't want to be the one who pushed her. I turned around and headed back home. The rain let up a bit and the sky grew brighter. Maybe we would have a sunny day after all.

When I got back to the cottage I walked into the middle of a hummingbird fight. Two ruby throated male hummingbirds were battling over exclusive rights to the feeder I set up for them on a tree overhanging the porch. They whirled and darted at each other inches from my face. I stepped back, trying to get out of their way, but they were so involved with each other I doubt they even noticed me. Finally, one drove the other off into the trees with a triumph whirl of his wings. He then came back and made a quick dart at me, surprising me so much I yelped. That sent him flying and me, too, straight into the house.

Just last week I had experienced some scary moments because of the hummingbirds on the front porch. There are two parts to my porch. The open side offers two old porch rockers placed so you can rest your feet on the top board of the porch railing while you look out over the lawn, fields and mountains. The corners of this section store firewood, garden tools and my basket packed with art supplies for my forays to the exquisite sites I try to paint. Overhead, hummingbird feeders, flowering plants and spider webs hang.

The other side of the porch is screened, the only defense against the black flies, midges, and mosquitoes that can make spring and summer in the mountains a difficult challenge. There a comfy old iron bed, painted white and pushed against the back wall and lined with pillows, provides me the place to write and watch and sometimes nap.

Last Tuesday I was headed for the screen porch, my mind on the next verse of a poem I was working on, when a sight stopped me dead in my tracks. Attached to the screen, about head high, was a tiny green iridescent body. A hummingbird had become trapped, her long beak thrust into the mesh of the screen, imprisoning her. She hung without moving and I stared at the little bird, struck dumb by her absence of hum and whirling wings. I hoped she was alive.

I gently pulled her beak free and she lay limp in the palm of my hand. Her emerald feathers caught the sun and flashed with beauty. The smallest of North American birds, the Ruby Throated Hummingbird has a long slender bill adapted for reaching deep into tubular flowers or hummingbird feeders like the one I hung at the other end of the porch. I put the feeder there to entice these fascinating birds from the gardens nearby so I could enjoy them up close. Their song is a rapid squeaky chirping, often made in flight. Their wing beat is so rapid it produces a humming sound even while feeding or hovering. Unbelievably, they can also fly backwards.

Their brilliant beauty, however, is only feather deep. They are fearless and extremely territorial. The males perch hidden near the feeder and will attack any other hummingbird that approaches. Sometimes these fights will go on for hours with neither bird able to drink from the feeder. Finally one will be vanquished or driven away and the victor comes and feeds in triumph.

The body lying in my hand lacked the bright red throat of the adult male, so I knew I held a female. Was she racing to feed her two babies, hatched from her small pea size white eggs, and distracted flew into the screen? Had another bird attacked her and driven her to her fate? Was the light at just the angle to render the screen invisible? How had she crashed into the obstacle on the other side of the porch?

I placed her tiny body into a fruit bowl lined with a linen napkin and set the bowl on the railing of the porch. I forced myself to cease stroking her soft feathers and left her alone, hoping she was only stunned and would come to consciousness on her own. I didn't know what else to do. I feared her neck was broken or she had died from shock and lack of oxygen after struggling to free herself from hanging from her beak at such an awkward angle for who knows how long. If she were still alive, I suspected my presence would only frighten her and speed up her metabolism. I didn't want her to die of a heart attack or shock from my touch, so I backed off and went into the house. I watched through the house door. Nothing. No head lifting, no wings beating.

I blamed myself for her death. I had hung the feeder and filled it crimson red with sugary syrup. I seduced her from her natural ways with the lure of easily attained artificial nourishment. I selfishly enjoyed the screens into which she had flown, thinking only of my own comfort and not about the hazard I was creating. How could I have been so unaware of, so ignorant, so careless about the little bird's needs? I grieved the loss of the whirling humming emerald flash. I grieved my part in her death.

Half an hour later I looked out the door again. The hummingbird was standing in the dish and whirling her wings. She flopped onto the railing and with a surge of energy hummed off into the trees. My heart lifted with her.

I then gathered two square leaded glass pieces that my friend Anne had created for me and attached them eye high to the deadly screen. No one, no bird, could miss the screen now. It was marked, artfully and beautifully, as a hazard. Then I moved the feeder off the porch to where it hangs now in the nearby tree.

Since then, I have noticed that the hummingbirds veer down and away after sipping at the feeder. They do not usually venture very close to the porch. At least not until today. Today I saw them as hostile gladiators, beautiful to look at but intent on killing their own kind. It was a sobering thought that brought my mind back to the body of the missing woman in the falls. Such a beautiful setting and such a terribly grotesque act, whether accident, suicide or murder.

After a shower, I finished my Down East Magazine reading and did a few chores that I had been neglecting. But the whole morning, ever since I woke up, on my walk and during my housework, my mind had been on the mystery of the missing woman, Josie, Alice and what was going on in Hummingbird Falls. I needed to find out more information. I called and left another message for Alice. It wasn't like her to ignore messages or not return a call. I would stop by her house again on my way to town. Finally, enough time had past so I could go to the pastry shop and learn if there were any new developments.

I drove first to Alice's place. Her house looked much the same as it had yesterday. Her car was parked as before. After repeated knocking, bell ringing and calling, I decided to walk to the back of the house. I peered in what windows I could, and everything looked tidy and normal. My knocking and calling at the back door brought no response either, so I returned to my car and headed for the pastry shop. I would ask around about Alice. Maybe someone knew where she was or what she was up to.

Again, the pastry shop parking lot was full. I pulled to the side, looking for a spot to park and instantly a huge black SUV eased up beside me. I noticed that the fenders were splashed with mud. I lowered my window, ready to explain why I was stopped.

"Morning pretty lady. Did you sleep well last night? If you didn't, you know you can call me anytime and I'll be there to do whatever I can to help."

"Thanks, Colby, I slept just fine. I'm just trying to find a parking spot. I'll move right along."

"No need to hurry, darling. Colby's gotcha covered. You just sit here as long as you want. By the way, did Josie stop by your place this morning?"

"No," I answered.

"Well, that's funny, because she told me she was going to. She said she had something she had to clear up with you. One of her little stories she told you. She thought you might have taken her seriously and she didn't want you to be misled."

"You saw Josie this morning?" I asked.

"Yes. I found her out wandering the roads, looking a sight all bundled up. She said she was going to see you."

"Well, I didn't see her. And I don't know about any little stories she might have told me either."

"If she does show up, Ellie, you call me." Colby removed his mirrored sunglasses and his bright blue eyes stared right into my eyes. "Got that? If you do see Josie, call me. I want to keep a watch on her.

I don't think she is doing too well. We might have to take her back to the hospital."

"Will do, Colby. Oh, there's someone backing out now. I'm going to grab that spot. See you later."

"You are right about that, Ellie. I will see you later. You can count on that."

I shivered off Colby's energy as I parked the car. I decided that I was going to talk to Dave about his assistant's less than professional manner. I was beginning to be bothered by his tone and the manner with which he spoke to me. It was subtle, but something was going on with Colby that made me nervous. The flirting was covering something ominous and I was going to do something about it, right after I had my coffee, turnover, and gossip.

Chapter 5

UMBRELLAS FILLED THE umbrella stand and the coat hooks were filled with dripping rain gear. The floor of the entry to the Pastry Shop was slippery with muddy wetness. I spotted Bonnie, Margaret and Sarah, who was taking an early lunch break from the Post Office and squeezed into their booth.

Sarah said, "Ellie, I'm glad you're here. We were just talking about what happened yesterday when you were here sitting with Bonnie and Pauline. Did you notice it too? Bonnie said that Pauline got upset and blushed bright red when folks were teasing about Colby's visiting the ladies."

"Yes, she did seem a little over reactive. What's that about?" I asked.

Bonnie jumped right in. "Pauline has had a thing for Colby ever since high school. They went out for a while, but Colby never could stick with just one woman for very long. Pauline said she would wait until he sowed his wild oats. She was sure he would eventually marry her.

She has been patiently waiting a long time, a very long time. But, when he started visiting Alice this year, she threw a fit."

Margaret continued, "She and Colby had a big fight in the library parking lot and I think the sound of that fight was heard all over town. You know how everything echoes around here."

"Everyone knew about it," Bonnie said. "Since then, Colby seems to have quieted things with Alice and Pauline told me Colby has been to see her a few times. Pauline seems to think if Colby stays away from Alice, she might have a chance again with him."

Margaret said, "I wouldn't be surprised if he was seeing them both. Even though Alice is old enough to be his mother, she has all the right assets, if you know what I mean. Plus, with all that land and her inheritance, she would be quite the catch. She's never married. Never seen anyone that I know of, except Mike Greeley now and then, until Colby started up with her."

"Pauline is so nice," I said. "Why would she want someone like Colby?"

"Just look at him," Margaret said. "And as quiet as Pauline is, and to be truthful, more than a little overweight, and so poor, she just isn't attractive to a lot of men. She told me that the library job hardly pays anything, and she is still trying to pay back her father's debts as well as her college loans. She worked all though college at the Inn on the Hill and still had to go into debt to get through. Colby's probably the only man to show her attention and she's not about to let him go."

"Well, why would Alice want him?" I asked. "I find it hard to believe that Alice would be attracted to a man like Colby. She never said anything about it to me and she isn't his type at all."

"Take another look at him," Margaret said. "He's gorgeous. And she's not getting any younger. Maybe she's been lonely. No family, except that loser of a brother. It's true; money doesn't always buy you happiness. You know Alice pretty well, Ellie. Does she seem happy to you?"

"Actually, I've always thought she was very pleasant, a good listener with a fine sense of humor. She's very smart and well educated.

I guess I noticed those qualities more, but now that you mention it, she has been rather down in the dumps lately, especially after a glass or two of wine."

I noticed the other women looking at one another and wondered if they were aware of Alice's occasional over indulgence in alcohol.

"I haven't talked with her for a while, maybe more than a week. Actually, not since her brother came. I've tried to reach her on the phone, but only get the machine. I stopped by her house but no one answered the door. Her car was there. I thought she might have gone off with her brother. Have either of you seen her?"

Sarah said, "Come to think of it, she hasn't been in for her mail for a while now. Her brother has a key to her mailbox and he's been in a couple of times, so they didn't go off on a trip together. But I haven't seen Alice. And I called her, too, and she never called me back."

Margaret just sat quietly, looking at us.

Then, it struck us all at the same time. We stared at each other. I knew what we were all thinking. Could Alice be the woman found at the bottom of the falls? No one wanted to be the one to say it.

But, if it were Alice, then what Josie had told me made sense. If Alice had been killed, than Josie must have seen it. I started to feel my adrenaline rise at the same time I felt scared to the bone. I didn't want to believe that my friend Alice was dead.

Bonnie jumped up. "Break time is over. I'm going to stop at the Police Station on my way back to work and talk to Dave about Alice. I am beginning to get a bad feeling about this."

After Bonnie left, Sarah mumbled a quick goodbye and wiping at her eyes, hurried back to the Post Office.

The hoards of tourists who visit Hummingbird Falls each year will never know the people, like Sarah, who work beneath the surface of this classic village. Postmaster Sarah Moody is one of those people who make the town work. She puts out the flag, brings in the mail, sets up the machines, breaks down the mail, closes out, order supplies, and finally brings in the flag. There is not much Sarah doesn't know about any of the 830 residents in this town. But unlike Bonnie and Debbie, Sarah is not much of a gossiper. She knows how to keep things to herself and seems to enjoy the trust of everyone as a result. She would be a good one for me to talk to about Josie. I could confide in her, get her opinion and then make a decision about what I should do. And either way I decided, I believed the information would be safe with Sarah.

There was a commotion at the door of the pastry shop. Dave Shaffer came in and stood at the counter facing the booths. A hush fell over the crowd. Not a clink of a spoon of the crunch of a cruller was heard.

"I've got some bad news, folks. The State Police just called me. They have identified the body found at the bottom of the falls."

Chapter 6

DAVE PAUSED AND rubbed his chin with a shaking hand. I could see that he was struggling to hold himself together. His eyes whelmed with tears.

"I'm sorry to say, it's Alice Foster."

A gasp went up from the crowd.

Dave continued, "I am calling for a town meeting to be held tomorrow night at the school cafeteria. I should have more of the details then. I still don't know how Alice died. The State Medical Examiner is working on that, but she promised me a preliminary report by tomorrow afternoon. So please spread the news about the meeting. The notice of the meeting will be on the radio and TV and I am putting flyers up all over town. But tell anyone you see. 7:30 pm starting time. And please, say a prayer for Alice. She was one of us, our friend for many years. She is going to be missed."

Dave turned his back and drew out his handkerchief. He had known Alice all his life. That she should die in such a bizarre way and at such a young age, only a few years older than he was, was devastating for him.

I was in shock. I think everyone was. It was one thing to talk about a body bashed and bruised at the bottom of the falls, but it was another thing to think about Alice's body, our friend, with her face unrecognizable, her body broken, dead in the falls we all swam in. No one could speak for a while. Then slowly people said their goodbyes and left the pastry shop. It was a sad day in Hummingbird Falls.

I left, too, determined now to talk to Sarah as soon as I could and then perhaps to tell Dave all that Josie had told me. I walked right over to the Post Office. On the front door was a notice announcing the meeting tomorrow night. I walked up to the counter and Sarah appeared from the sorting room. She had been crying.

"It's so terrible, Ellie. Poor Alice. What could have happened to her? She was one of my dearest friends. I should have checked up on her this week. I normally would have seen her everyday, when she came for her mail, but her brother was here and I didn't want to interfere, or get in the way. It has been thirteen years since they have seen each other and I figured they had a lot of healing to do. Oh, Alice is gone. I don't believe it."

Sarah's sadness brought on my own. I started to well up and had to bite my tongue to keep myself together. "I am so sorry, Sarah. We've all lost a friend. It's just beyond belief. Maybe we'll learn some more at the meeting. For now, I guess we just have to begin to learn how to deal with our loss. This is so terrible. Our dear Alice. I can't believe she's gone. I am just so very, very sad."

I knew my words were totally inadequate. What could I say? Nothing would change the fact that Alice was dead. I knew that from my own experience. The sympathetic words people tried to soothe me with after Chris died, were meaningless to me at first. Only years later, could I begin to understand what those kind words intended. But perhaps I could help to shed some light on how Alice had died.

So, I took a deep breath and said, "Sarah, I have something I want to talk to you about. Something that may have to do with Alice's death. Could we get together after you finish work today? Say around 5:30? And could we meet at your house so we have some privacy? Would that be okay?"

Sarah stopped crying and looked at me with reddened eyes. "What do you mean, Ellie? What do you know?"

"I think it is better if we talk about it in private. You never know when someone is going to come in here and I need to keep this information confidential between you and me. Someone else's safety may depend on keeping what I know secret. I'll explain it all, I promise. Can I come to your house at 5:30?"

"Yes, certainly, please. I'll do anything that might help find out what happened to Alice."

Just then the door opened and a tourist with a package to mail came in and stood right behind me.

"I'll see you later," I said and left to go to Dave's office.

Chapter 7

I ARRIVED AT the Hummingbird Falls Police Office, located in the basement of the Town Hall, just after Dave did. All six feet of him looked frazzled. His tan face was lined with worry, his gray hair falling into his face rather than combed neatly back as usual, and his blue eyes darted around his small office as if searching for something lost.

Dave said, "Mind if I sit, Ellie? I'm bushed. Finding out it was Alice has just ripped my heart. She was such a wonderful woman. Alice was one of Mary and my best friends for years. And I have to find out what happened to her." He pushed his lean frame back in the imitation black leather chair and stared at the ceiling.

"By the way, I am glad you came by. I have been meaning to talk to you. I think you can help me in a special way. I don't want to talk about it here in the office, but will you come to my home tonight for dinner and we can talk then?"

My curiosity was raised sky high, but Dave had made it clear he didn't want to talk about it in the office. So, I pushed the information I was going to share aside and I only said, "I'd love to come to dinner. I haven't had a chance to see Mary except in the grocery store between the cauliflower and the shrimp sauce. So, it will be a chance to catch up. And it will feel good to be with friends tonight. Sometimes it helps just to be with someone. I don't want to be home alone with my thoughts and sorrows all night. What time and what can I bring?"

"Just come around 7:00. I should be done here by then. And just bring yourself. You know how Mary loves to cook for guests. She would probably be insulted if you tried to add anything to her menu, even if you were well intended."

Dave paused. "I appreciate it Ellie."

"Likewise," I said.

"Now I have to make some calls, but did you come in for more than to say hello?"

"I did, Dave." I quickly shifted priorities, not wanting to bring up Josie until later. "It's a bit awkward and I don't want to stir up trouble, but I want to talk to you about Colby."

Dave groaned. "I bet I know just what you're going to say. I had another woman in here today, who is staying over at the Waterford Inn. She said Colby was fresh to her, suggestive. Am I on the right trail?"

"Close, Dave. He's been flirty, flattering and making some inappropriate, completely non-professional comments. Maybe he's just young or is trying to be friendly, but it doesn't go over well with me. I feel like he has some agenda, wants something from me, but I don't know what. And he seems obsessive about Josie. Sometimes I feel nervous around him."

"I hear you, Ellie. I haven't a clue what the Josie thing is about, but I'll ask him. I'm going to speak to him about the inappropriate stuff as well. I'll do it this afternoon, I assure you. If he ever acts or speaks to you in that way again, you let me know. I'll suspend him if I hear any more complaints like this. I know everyone likes to tease him, like he is the Casanova of Hummingbird Falls, but he has obviously gone too far.

Don't worry about it. I'll take care of it. Now, I do have to make those calls. I'll see you tonight at 7."

"Thanks Dave. I know you wouldn't want something like this to be going on behind your back. You take this job and the reputation of the police force seriously. I respect that and yes, I will see you at 7."

That gave me enough time to meet with Sarah at 5:30 and still be at Dave and Mary's at 7. It would be a busy night, but hopefully one full of information and perhaps some resolution. Until then, I had plenty to do. I had been neglecting my writing and painting and I needed some time alone to remember and eulogize Alice.

During my ride up the mountain I recalled how Alice and I had met and become friends. My friendship with Alice began the first summer I came to Hummingbird Falls. I met her at the gallery where I was speaking to Margaret about selling some of my paintings. Alice came in and looked at the paintings and told Margaret she would be a fool not to take all of them on commission. Our friendship was sealed right there. I left the gallery with Alice and we went to the pastry shop and had coffee and turnovers and talked about ourselves. I learned that Alice had lost her mother to cancer at a young age. When her father remarried and her half brother James was born, she had felt abandoned and alone. Later on, she went to a mid-east college, fell in love and was devastated in her early twenties by her fiancé deserting her. She disappeared for a while, as she put it, touring Europe by herself. Later she returned to school, received a M.A. in Art History and was continuing on to earn a Ph.D. with hopes of teaching at the college level. Then her father developed cancer and she was needed at home. Her brother, James, who was quite a few years younger than she, had left home shortly after he graduated from high school, after a terrible scene in which his parents had accused him of having a gambling addiction. They had discovered that he stolen and sold a great many heirlooms from the family estate. In addition, James calimed he owed $10,000 to some very shady characters who were threatening him and his family if he didn't pay up. Alice's parents paid the loan off, and told James they didn't want to see him again until he was in recovery from his addiction. He left and never returned, not even for the funeral of his father. Shortly following her father's death, Alice's stepmother started slowly deteriorating, suffering from cardiac disease. Her stepmother lingered several years and then died. James didn't show up for her funeral either. That was eight years ago, and since then Alice lived in their big house, alone.

I told her all about me, too. How I was happy growing up an only child until my parent's fatal car accident when I was only seven. I was taken in by my mean old Aunt Jennifer and escaped my depression by eating until I was an obese teenager just a step from suicide. I managed to get admitted to college, started to get counseling and then went on to graduate school. I spoke of my teaching job, marriage, children, the death of Chris, to whom I was happily married for 18 years, and how I found myself here in Hummingbird Falls. I told her how writing, painting and gardening filled my soul and sent my spirit soaring and had helped with my healing. I told her my dream of moving to Hummingbird Falls year round, and that so far I hadn't been able to find anything I could afford. She listened attentively.

When the shop closed, Alice invited me over to her home for drinks and dinner and I accepted and we continued telling the tales of ourselves. We talked about literature, art, music, and all the things we loved. We found we had much in common and we had been friends ever since. That is until now, now that she was dead. I didn't know what I would do without her. I imagined that many in Hummingbird Falls felt the same way. She was a wonderful woman and she would be missed.

I wondered who would arrange for Alice's funeral service. I decided to call her number and ask for her brother when I got back to the cottage. James and I had never met, but he probably wasn't on speaking terms with many of the people in town since he had been gone for thirteen years. And, I figured, anyone would want help with arranging a funeral service for a relative. I was a little wary about contacting him because of all the talk I had heard about him, but I would have to take that chance for the sake of my friendship with Alice. How could he get angry at me for wanting to help? But, then again, I didn't know what he was capable of doing. I hoped my call wouldn't make me next on his list, that is, if he had a list, if Alice had been murdered, and if he were the one who had killed his sister.

Chapter 8

AS I PULLED into the cottage driveway, I noticed that the rain had flattened my daffodils and the early irises that were shooting up in the far wet corner of the yard. I walked through the sodden grass with the intention of picking a few of the daffodils to bring inside. I started to pass by the Siberian Irises that Mike had let me transplant from the overgrown garden at the back of his house. I love irises and was thrilled to accept his offer. His irises had been planted decades ago by his grandmother and were always a spring experience as they spread their lush purple above the green grasses.

I looked down to where I had so lovingly and carefully dug in the tubers and roots last fall. I anxiously searched for the first blooms. I had been excited when the stalks, musky green blue flat swords growing up from the ground in early spring, first showed. I watched with joy as the stem arose from the center of the stalks into the sun and air. And now I hoped to see buds ready to bloom.

At the very tip of the stems tiny long pointed buds, tightly closed, had formed. As I looked closer, I noticed a fine purple line along the length of each bud. I was so excited. The flowers were only a breath away from blooming. Then I looked again. At the tip of the bud extruded what looked like a wilted, blackened petal, faintly purple. Maybe the petal could have been the beginnings of an Iris flower, but something was very wrong. Then I noticed that all the buds were in this condition. They were dying before blooming. The buds' green covers were caskets, not cradles. Death lurked everywhere in what seemed to be a perfect birthing place for the vulnerable buds.

I was devastated. Then I grew angry. What had happened? What was killing my iris that I had tended so carefully and awaited for so long? I would find out. Tentatively, I broke off a bud and examined it. The lovely green casing was swollen with the growing flower inside, but there were no signs of wormholes, no nibbling of caterpillars, no web of spider mites, droppings of larvae or clutch of aphids. In fact, the bud looked beautiful, except for the dried up, blackened petal partially born from the opening at the tip of the bud. I examined the leaves. They were slightly ragged looking with signs of sap oozing out. I picked a stem and examined it. Perfectly green and healthy on the outside. And yet, it felt hollow. Hmm. Were iris stems supposed to be hollow?

I slogged my way back to the porch to get out of the rain and took my handy Swiss Army knife out of my pocket. I cut the stem carefully from bottom to top. Nothing but a little tunnel, clean and clear. And then I sliced through the bud, severing it in half. And there they were. Pinkish white worms, plump and squirmy. They were everywhere inside what was supposed to be my lovely Iris flower. They were twitching their way through rotten slimy brown Iris petals, leaving behind foul smelling excrement.

The budding of the Iris, soft and fuzzy deep purple, flecked here and there with yellow and white was destroyed. I shuddered with disgust at these maggoty looking murderers that had so viciously slaughtered my flowers. I put the autopsied bud on a rock and crushed it beneath my shoe until it was a mash of vegetation and worm.

I walked back down to the Iris bed and dug up the tuberous bulb, called the rhizome, all that was left of that Iris plant. It was firm and seemed perfectly healthy too. But under my knife, I discovered more of the white wigglers nesting in the fiber of the bulb, probably just arrived from their trip from the destroyed bud down the stem tunnel. I killed them too.

Then I ran and got my *Guide to Common Insects*, tucked back on the shelf that holds my gardening books. I looked in the index and there it was: The Iris Borer. I quickly read up on its life history, prevention and control. I was dismayed to learn that an adult moth can lay up to

1,000 eggs in her life time, depositing them in the fall in the dried iris leaves. The eggs hatch during April and May and then larvae begin to eat the young iris leaves. The larvae bore into the leaves and mine upwards into the forming flowers and downwards toward the rhizome, causing soft rot. Eventually the larvas leave the iris and burrow into the soil, and enter the pupa stage. After two or three weeks the iris borer moth emerges and lays her eggs, the vicious cycle complete.

The best organic prevention is removing and destroying the previous year's dead foliage before April. It was too late now. The other non-pesticide alternative was to kill them by hand, squeezing the bug-ridden leaves between the fingers and thumb, or by destroying the infested rhizome itself, resulting in the loss of that particular iris plant. I pictured myself out in the large bed of iris, squishing thousands of plump writhing worms between my fingers. I gagged at the thought. I decided that I would put it out of my mind for now and phone James Foster instead. Somehow, calling him didn't seem as bad as hand killing borers in the pouring rain.

I called. The line was busy. I called periodically and the line continued to be busy. Finally, I got through. I explained I was one of Alice's friends and said I would be honored to help with her memorial service.

"There aren't going to be any services," James answered. "She is going to be cremated and that's it."

"But James, people in town loved her. They'll want a service to celebrate her life. She meant a great deal to this town."

"Well, I'm the next of kin and I get to decide what is and what isn't happening. If you want to have a service, then go ahead. I'm having her cremated and that's all I'm going to do."

"What are you doing with the ashes?" I asked.

He paused. "I haven't thought about that yet. I suppose you can have them for the service if you wish."

"I do wish, James. Can you tell me why you don't want a service? Is something wrong?"

"Yeah, something's wrong. Something has been wrong in this family for a long time. But that isn't any of your business or anyone else's. And I don't want to be on display as the so called bad boy of Hummingbird Falls. I know what everyone's thinking. They think I killed my own sister. Well, let them prove it. I finished with this town a long time ago and I'll be out of here as soon as I can. You can pick the ashes up at the crematorium in Greenberg. That's all I have to say. Goodbye."

I put the phone down in a daze. What was James' problem? He certainly didn't sound like a grieving brother. But being separated from his half-sister for thirteen years didn't seem like the behavior of a very loving brother either. I decided I would ask Sarah about him, too.

I was too upset to paint or write, and although I wanted to talk with my children and share my sorrow with them, they would still be at work. I decided I would wait until later when I could actual interact with them rather than leave a message. They had been so fond of Alice, too.

So I filled the tub with warm bubbly bath water and soaked myself until I felt better and lay down in bed for just a short while. I awoke several hours later, startled that it was 5:00. I had better hurry to make my appointment with Sarah.

Sarah was waiting for me on the front porch of her lovely old bungalow which was surrounded by perennial gardens and handsome huge pines, white birch and flowering crab apple trees. Living her life alone hadn't seemed to diminish her in any way. She was tall and vibrant, full of energy. Although her face was wrinkled and her gray hair forever tied up in a tight bun, she wore stylish classic clothing and always looked like she stepped out of a fashion magazine. I didn't know much about Sarah's personal life. I hadn't really moved beyond the friendly acquaintance stage with her, as I had with Alice, Margaret, Mike, and Dave and Mary. She was very busy with the Post Office and the Historical Society. I hadn't seen her at church, but she attended most social functions in town. Everyone knew her and most seemed to like her. I hadn't ever heard any gossip about her which in this small town was surprising.

Either she was perfect or she held some power over the village rumor mongers. I wondered what her personal history would add to the impression I had. Maybe she would reveal some intimacies from her past if we got to know each other more personally.

She had a tall glass of ice tea with a sprig of mint peeping over the top all ready for me. I hugged her hello and asked, "How are you doing, Sarah?"

"Not too well. It was so hard at work. Everyone came in and all day long it was talk, talk, talk about Alice. So I had to go over it again and again. The questions of why and how she died. The awful allegations that she killed herself. That's the worst. Alice would never kill herself. Unless something happened with her brother that drove her to it. I wouldn't put it past him. But no, even then, she wouldn't kill herself. Even though she has been depressed lately she wouldn't commit suicide. It's just not like her."

"I know. I agree," I said. "And I don't think Alice would slip into the falls either. She knew the falls as well as anyone. She wouldn't have had an accident. And if she did slip in by mistake, she knew where the strong currents ran and how to side swim out of them. I have seen her do that a thousand times."

Sarah said, "Then we can only assume someone put her into the falls, or threw her in. She was murdered. I'd bet my life on it. But who would do such a thing?"

"That's just what I wanted to talk to you about, Sarah. I had a visitor two nights ago and I want to tell you about it and get your advice. But you must swear complete confidentiality. You can't talk about what I'm going to tell you to anyone because it might mean someone else will be in trouble. Can you promise me you won't say anything?"

Sarah thought for a minute. She took a sip of tea. "It's hard to promise not to say anything about something you don't know yet. But if it helps to catch Alice's killer, then, yes, I promise." She held up her hand in a kind of Girl Scout sign of truthfulness.

"The night before last," I started off. "Two nights ago, Josie visited me around 10:30. I was just about to go to bed. She startled me.

She was all dressed up in tons of clothes and wanted me to keep the lights off, so 'they' wouldn't see her."

"That sounds like Josie when she isn't taking her meds," Sarah said.

"Well, she was pretty wound up." I hesitated. Then I blurted it out. "She told me that she saw Alice being killed."

"What?" Sarah said. "How could she have known that? Dave only found out for sure this morning."

"I know," I said. "But I didn't know that two nights ago. And even more astonishing, Josie said she saw who did it, who killed Alice."

"Who?" Sarah gasped.

"She didn't say. She started to get all paranoid when I said we should call the police and she wouldn't say anything more except that it was a mistake to tell me and that no one would believe her anyway. I have to admit; I really didn't believe her either. After all, I didn't know about Alice then."

"What happened next?"

"She got so upset she pulled a big knife out and said I had to be eliminated from some plan she had. I was scared. I know she would never hurt anyone, or at least that is what everyone says, but when you are facing an upset woman wielding a big butcher knife, terror wipes out all reason. I'm afraid I just wanted to get her out of my house and tricked her into leaving. I haven't seen her since."

"Oh my," Sarah whispered.

"And that's why I wanted to talk to you, to get some advice from you since you know Josie better than I do. Could she be telling the truth? Did she see Alice killed? If I report this to Dave, is he apt to think she's the killer? Could she have killed Alice? Why would she tell me she saw the killer but not tell me who it was? I need your help, Sarah. Should I believe Josie and go to Dave or should I just keep quiet?"

"Wow. This is a tough one. I know Josie makes up some super stories and that no one really believes what she says anymore. So, Dave is likely to dismiss it all as just one more of her paranoid stories. But she did know about Alice. She could have just said her name and it is a coincidence that it really was Alice who was killed, but I doubt it. Somehow, she knew it was Alice. On the other hand, if it gets around that Josie saw the killer, then the murderer will try to kill her too, I suspect, to eliminate her as an eyewitness. Although I don't think she would be a very credible witness on the stand."

I asked, "Could she have done it herself and that's why she knew it was Alice's body that had been found?"

"No," answered Sarah. "Definitely not. She's against violence of any kind. She doesn't even kill black flies or mosquitoes. That's why she wears that awful beekeeper net and covers herself from head to toe. She wants to make sure she doesn't kill any bugs by accidentally slapping at them. I don't know about the butcher knife. That's a new behavior and maybe she's just really scared and feels she needs it for protection. But she might have been down by the falls late at night or early in the morning and saw Alice's body before any one else did. Then being upset about it, she might have made up the part about seeing the killer too. But I am pretty sure she didn't have anything to do with it herself."

Sarah continued, "And I don't think Dave will suspect her either. But he'll have to talk to her, and she'll resist. She's terrified of the police. They'll have to break into her house to question her or search for her out in the woods. She'll go wild. It could take days to find her. And that would be really hard for Josie. Without food and water and her meds she would decompensate quickly. She isn't that healthy to begin with. If they try to take her into the Police Station to question her she will probably be driven right into another hospital stay. So telling Dave is just about a guarantee for disaster for Josie."

"But if we don't tell him," I started.

"Right," Sarah interrupted. "If we don't tell him then we have to talk to her ourselves and try to get the truth out of her and then investigate until we have enough evidence to support Josie's statement and then bring it all to Dave in one package that he can't ignore."

"That's it, Sarah," I said. "We will investigate ourselves, just you and me. Josie knows us both pretty well and would be more likely to talk with us. We just have to figure out a way to convince her we're on her side, so she'll tell us everything. Then, we check out the killer and get the goods on him. Perfect. We can do that, I'm sure. If Miss Marple can solve mysteries, then so can we."

Sarah frowned at me. "Don't get carried away, Ellie. I am counting on your steady calmness in all this. Remember, this isn't a TV series. A real woman, our Alice, was really killed dead, and right here. So, someone is actually a murderer, not pretend. That means we have to be very careful, too."

Knocked down a notch, I regained my usual analytical frame of mind. "Okay. What's our plan?"

Sarah smiled. "That's more like it. One, we don't tell Dave until we have something to tell him. Agreed?"

"Agreed," I said.

"Two, we have to talk to Josie."

"Right. When? I have to go over to Dave and Mary's tonight for supper. I should be through there by 9:00, I'm sure. Can we meet at my house at 9:30 and go to Josie's from there? Her house is just up the road a couple of miles."

"Don't you think that might be a little dangerous, Ellie? It will be pitch dark by then. No one else around. Couldn't we go during the day? It might be less scary."

"I think we have to talk to her right away, before anything else happens, Sarah. I don't want to be responsible for holding on to Josie's information about seeing Alice murdered any longer than I have to. I want to get this settled tonight so I can tell Dave."

"I guess you are right, but I'm afraid it might be a little too spooky for me."

"I'll be right by your side, Sarah. Don't worry. Nothing will happen to us."

"I hope you're right, Ellie. Okay. But let's make sure we have a good flashlight. That's number three. We meet at your house tonight at 9:30 and drive up to Josie's. Now what about Four? What's our approach going to be?"

"Good question," I said. "Well, she came to me before. Maybe I can say I want to help her and I brought you along because I knew she would trust you."

"That might work, or she could still be upset with you. I don't want any knife play. I could say I came to visit her and brought her mail because she hadn't been in to get it for a while. And I brought you because, because…"

"You brought me because you knew I was her friend and, and, well, you were afraid to be out so late on her dark road by yourself, so you stopped to pick me up," I finished her sentence with an excited yell.

"Good, but curb that enthusiasm, Ellie. You have to keep calm. Now, we have one, two, three and four. I guess we will come up with the rest when we hear what she has to say. You could start that off once we get in. Something like that you have wanted to help her, and so on. And I could play dumb and ask with what and that should loosen things up a bit. Josie does like to talk, so if we just give her starters, she should take over."

I stood and hugged Sarah. "I'm off to Dave and Mary's now. I think we have a great plan. Thanks so much Sarah. I promise I'll stay composed. I just got a little carried away. See you later."

"I'll be at your house at 9:30," Sarah said. "I feel better that I'm doing something for Alice, and not just weeping about her. Thanks, Ellie."

Chapter 9

MARY IS A wonderful cook and the dinner she fixed was superb. We chatted about Hummingbird Falls' gossip through the corn chowder, and mixed green salad. We shared memories of summers past during the marinated brook trout fillets, sides of oven roasted baby red potatoes, fresh green peas from the garden and pickled beets. We recalled our happy experiences with Alice as we drank coffee and devoured cherry pie and vanilla ice cream. Then Mary said she would refill our coffee cups and we could take them out to the front screen porch while she did the dishes and tidied up the kitchen. Clearly, she knew Dave wanted to talk to me in private.

We settled on the porch, leaving the lights off. The thick cushions on the old wicker furniture were easy to sit in, especially after such a huge and well-enjoyed meal. Dave got right to it.

"You know I wanted to talk to you, Ellie. I have been thinking about this ever since I found out that Alice was the woman who had gone over the falls. Something isn't right about this whole matter. I should know more about the cause of her death tomorrow, before the meeting, but even then, I think I'm going to need some help. I don't think Alice had an accident. I don't think she committed suicide. I think she was murdered. That's where you come in."

"Me? How can I help you, Dave? I agree with you that Alice most likely was murdered, but what can I do?"

"Ellie, I have lived here all my life. That gives me a great advantage because I know everybody and they know me. But in a case like this, where one of our own is found dead, and it may be by foul means, then I don't start clean with folks. Do you know what I mean? I have biases because I know so much. In a city, the cops don't know all the relatives, the business, the rumors, and the relationship, financial, history or sex difficulties of both the deceased and the suspects. They start clean and see what facts build into a case. Here, I have all the facts about everyone already and that confuses the picture. I could pass the case on to the State Police, but I don't want to. It is our business and it should be up to us to take care of it. At least, that's the way I look at it."

"I understand what you are saying, Dave, and I agree. But where do I fit in?"

"I'm getting to that, Ellie. You're our friend. You're one of us in a way, but not one of us in another. I don't mean to be insulting to you. But you've been here only 13-15 years, right?"

"Actually, I have been coming here only 10 years, Dave."

"Boy, seemed longer to me. Anyway, we all know you and trust you and you know us and trust us, I hope. But you haven't grown up with us. You don't know all the stuff that went on before, the stuff that complicates this case. So, you might be able to see some things more clearly than I can. I want you to be my consultant in this case. I will share certain information with you that you must keep to yourself. No telling anyone else, not even Colby. He's young and brash, sometimes. By the way, I talked to him about his unbecoming behavior. If you experience any more of that attitude, let me know immediately. He's sometimes pretty immature. I don't think he's mature enough yet to be fully involved with some of the undercover investigations. Besides he will be kept busy with running down all the tips, tourists, and taking care of the other police business that comes up. And you have experience with communication and people skills. You can go around and talk to people, Ellie, and get information that I probably couldn't or wouldn't think of to ask because I think I know it all anyway."

I was getting excited. "Let me see if I get this, Dave. You will tell me some clue or fact that came up in the investigation and you want me to talk to people who could have had something to do with Alice's death. In those conversations I try to get the person talking about their possible connection to that evidence and then come and tell you what it is I learned."

"Yes, that's about it. Now, I know it may sound rather sneaky, and, really it is, so I wouldn't blame you if you'd rather not. It isn't really betraying the people you know. If you do find out information that leads to solving the case, then you have done everyone a good deed, even if it's done in sort of a backhanded way. But it's up to you."

I thought for a moment. Dave didn't know, but I was already doing exactly what he was asking. I was talking to Sarah and Josie about information on Alice's death. If I also got more information from Dave, then it would be even easier for me to put things together and help bring closure to this case.

"Dave, I would be happy to help you. Just tell me what you want me to do or with whom you want me to talk and I'll do my best. You can count on me."

"Thanks Ellie. I know it's asking a lot and I really appreciate your help. I need someone like you that I can trust. We can probably start tomorrow. When I get the Medical Examiners report, I'll hold certain things back from the public. That's pretty standard. Investigators are supposed to do that to help with the case. It keeps the crazies from claiming credit for the death, and often when investigators question suspects, the suspect will give up certain information that has been withheld, proving that they were the perpetrators, since no one else would have known that particular fact. Some things only the killer would know. So, I will tell you some of the details I hold back and you can use that knowledge in your conversations."

"It sounds like you know what you're doing, Dave. I'll do my best. Should I call you tomorrow?"

"Ellie, just so you know. This is only the second homicide case I've handled. First one was the Wilson's. I messed that up bad. I made a lot of mistakes that I really regret. I never brought the killer to trial. I never even had a major suspect besides Callie Wilson, the teenage daughter. The gun had Callie's fingerprints on it. I was sure she had killed her parents and ran off to some big city and just disappeared. But why? I never could really understand her motive, other than that her parents were very strict with her. That case just bewildered me. Besides the dead parents and the fingerprints on the gun and the missing girl, I had nothing. Then almost a year later some kid found a skull up by Adder Creek. Turned out to be Callie Wilson's. At least that told us Callie wasn't missing any longer and most likely wasn't the murderer. We didn't have all the forensics and computer technology then that we have today. But still, that family deserved better. And, I am not going to let that happen again. I will find Alice's killer. So, I am really going to try to follow the book on this one. Get help when I can and pray that it will all come out right in the end. I'll call you when I have more to go on. In the meantime, just carry on as you normally would."

"Thanks for telling me that, Dave," I said. "I have been hearing a lot of talk about the Wilson case. I'm willing to bet no one could have found the murderer in that case. From what I understand there were no clues, no evidence, no witnesses. I'm sure you did all that anyone could to solve it."

Dave frowned. "Yes, but I didn't solve it. I have kept that case file on my desk for thirteen years and haven't got any closer today than I was then. I won't let that happened this time." Dave banged his fist on the arm of the chair. "Poor Alice. I will find out who killed her if it's the last thing I do."

I tried to distract Dave from his anger and self blame. "I'm trying to get a group together to help with Alice's service. I talked with her brother and he sounds like a nasty guy. I haven't heard one good word about him. He won't even give her a memorial service. I think you should check him out. I bet he had something to do with Alice's death. At least he might know something that happened around the time of her death."

"I already called him," Dave said. "He's agreed to talk with me, but not until we release the information about what happened to Alice. He said he knows nothing about it. He went to bed early and is a sound sleeper. He didn't hear anything unusual. She just wasn't there when he got up in the morning. He thought she might be visiting friends."

"Well, he's releasing her body to the crematorium and that's as much as he would tell me when I called him today. He said we could pick up the ashes and do with them what we want. What a terrible man. How could he be so uncaring? Anyway, I thought a nice simple celebration of her life in the Little Church would be what she would want. Do you know when her body will be released?"

"No. If I were you, I would go ahead and plan the memorial anyway. Forget about James. We all have. After the way he treated his parents and Alice? He doesn't deserve to be called next of kin. Anyway, having the ashes there doesn't really matter, does it? It would be good for the town if we had the service as soon as possible. Then we could get on with mourning our loss."

"Alright, I'll move ahead then with planning the service. That will help, too, in that I'll have to contact a lot of people about the plans and that will give them a chance to talk about what's on their minds. Maybe I'll pick up some clues that way. I want to say goodbye to Mary and then be on my way. I'll see you at the meeting tomorrow night, Dave."

"Yep, I imagine everyone will be there. Could be interesting."

I hugged Mary goodnight and thanked her for the delicious dinner and accepted her recipe for marinated brook trout and a piece of the cherry pie to take home with me. I could probably use a snack for the energy I would need for my next adventure tonight. Bedtime seemed far away. Sarah and I had to talk to Josie tonight if at all possible and that could be tricky. Visions of butcher knives danced through my mind as I began the long dark trip up the mountain to my cottage and the rendezvous with Sarah.

Mary's Marinated Brook Trout

4(4-ounce trout fillets)
¼ cup peanut oil
2 tablespoons soy sauce
2 tablespoons balsamic vinegar
2 tablespoons chopped green onions
1 ½ teaspoons brown sugar
1 clove garlic, finely minced
¾ teaspoon ground ginger
½ teaspoon dried red pepper flakes
½ teaspoon sesame oil
Salt and freshly ground pepper to taste

1. Combine peanut oil, soy sauce, balsamic vinegar, green onions, garlic, brown sugar, ginger, red peppers and sesame oil.
2. Place fish in a shallow glass dish, and pour marinade over fish. Cover with plastic wrap and refrigerate for 20 minutes.

3. Preheat barbecue or gas grill. Oil the grill rack, and adjust height about 5 inches from coals.
4. Remove fish from marinade and place on grill. Cook until fish flakes easily, turning once to brown both sides. Season with salt and pepper to taste. Serve immediately.

Makes 4 servings

Chapter 10

AFTER A BRIEF discussion about the possible dangers of walking to Josie's house from the main road, Sarah and I left my car at the end of Josie's road. Although it would be more secure and certainly easier if we drove down the dirt road, we didn't want Josie to hear the engine and take off into the woods. If at all possible we wanted to talk with her inside her home where we had a little more control over preventing her from escaping from us.

The night sky was gloomy with looming thunderheads. Josie's road was dark and downright spooky. Huge trees formed an arch over the old dirt road and blocked out whatever light might have escaped the threatening clouds, which hid the stars and promised more rain before long. My small flashlight was almost useless, but by holding it right in front of us, we did manage to stay on the dirt road and make it around the bend to where Josie's house stood. The house was completely dark, a black shadow against the blacker woods in back of it.

Sarah and I walked slower and tried to be even quieter. We tiptoed up the porch stairs, winching at each squeak and creak we made. We looked at each other, knowing that if Josie were here she had to have heard us, so we started talking out loud to each other to let her know whom we were and our purpose in coming there.

"Gee Ellie; it sure is dark out here in the woods. If you hadn't had a flashlight I don't know if we could have found Josie's house."

"Yes, Sarah. It is so good of you to bring her mail all the way out here. I am sure glad you stopped by to pick me up, so you wouldn't be out here alone in the dark. Can't be too careful, you know."

"I hope we don't scare Josie, by just showing up like this," Sarah said quite loudly. "You know she doesn't have a phone so we couldn't warn her in advance that we were coming."

"Oh Sarah," I said just short of yelling. "Josie knows we are her good friends. She wouldn't be scared of us. She knows we are just trying to help."

I was about ready to end this fiasco when a voice whispered from the bushes.

"Keep your voices down. Sound travels out here and I don't want anyone to hear us talking. What are you doing here? I don't need any help."

"Can we come inside, Josie? The bugs are eating us alive," I said.

"I don't know," Josie answered. "I have to think about it."

"I have your mail, Josie," Sarah said. "There is quite a bit of it and one looks like your check. You want to look at that, don't you?"

"Okay. Okay. You can come in. You don't have any recorders on you, do you? No metal antennas? I won't have transcribers in my house. I've worked hard to demagnetize everything, so no metals."

"I'll leave my watch on the porch railing," I said. "Otherwise, everything I have on is natural fiber."

"Me, too," said Sarah. "Even my crowns are porcelain and they cost a pretty penny, too."

I said under my breath, "We don't have to go that far, Sarah." Leaving the flashlight and our watches on the railing, we followed Josie into her house. It was too dark to see my hand before my face.

Josie said, "Follow me. We will go to the back screen porch. That way the bugs won't get you and I can hear if any cars come my way. I have to be careful. I have to be very careful. The last car that came down here wanted to hurt me. I know he did. I watched him from the bushes and he had his gun out ready to shoot me. Wicked police."

I nudged Sarah who was plastered right up next to me as we baby stepped our way through the dark, following the sound of Josie's shuffling steps. I reminded myself to tell her about the speeding police SUV I saw this morning on my walk. I wondered if this was to whom Josie was referring.

Suddenly we were stepping down onto the back porch. There was a little more light or else my eyes were adjusting slowly to the darkness and I could make out Josie and Sarah's silhouettes.

"Sit down on the cushions," Josie said as she disappeared from view.

Squatting down slowly, I reached out my hand and felt a cushion next to me. I sat on it. I heard Sarah do the same.

"Could we have some light so you can read your mail, Josie?" Sarah said.

"I'll read it tomorrow," Josie said. "No light. They will see it."

"Who will see it, Josie?" Sarah asked.

"The ones who killed her," Josie answered. "I saw it all, you know. I saw everything and now I'm going to be next if I don't watch out. You could be next, too."

"Who did you see, Josie?" Sarah whispered.

"Why should I tell you?" Josie answered.

"Because we could help you," I said.

"Help me how?" Josie said.

I was stumped there, but Sarah took up the conversation and said, "If you tell us the whole story, what you saw and who you saw, Ellie and I can go and get evidence to prove that you are right. Then poor Alice will be avenged and none of us will be in danger anymore. Doesn't that make sense, Josie?"

"I have to think about that," Josie said.

Several minutes passed in the dark. I could hear the crickets and the peepers singing away and the rustle of the leaves as the wind began to pick up. The storm would be on us in no time and I didn't relish walking back to the car in the thunder and lightning and drenching downpour that was bound to come soon.

"Are you still thinking, Josie?" I asked.

"You interrupted me," she said. "Now I have to start all over again."

My back was killing me. Sitting on those cushions on the floor with nothing to lean against brought back painful memories of when I was trying to learn how to meditate, clear my mind and work on patience. My major distraction was not my mind, but my back, which refused to cooperate with my newfound interest. Now, I wanted to move, stand up, stretch, anything that would relieve the aching strain. I counted to one hundred again. Still no response from Josie. How did Sarah manage to remain so still? Probably had to do with postal training or long hours of bending over bins of mail.

Josie finally spoke. "I was out walking, very early in the morning, two days ago. I like to walk when no one's around and there aren't any cars in the road. I walked past your place, Ellie. I stop by there most evenings to check on you and make sure all is well. Everything looked safe that morning, so I went on. I decided to walk down to the falls. There had been so much rain that I knew they would be a sight in the dark. The white water would show up no matter how dark and that's a pretty sight. As I got closer, I couldn't hear anything but the water crashing against the rocks. You know how it is during ice melt in the spring. It was at least that loud. I never heard the car coming until the last moment."

I opened my big mouth. "What car?"

Josie fell silent.

I waited a few minutes and then said, "I'm sorry, Josie. I won't interrupt you again."

Josie didn't answer.

Sarah said, "Josie, she didn't mean it. She's just anxious to help. Tell me. I'm listening and I didn't interrupt. Tell me the story."

"I didn't hear the car until the last moment, but I saw the headlights in enough time to jump off the road and into the bushes. The car was coming from Alice's way and driving very fast toward the upper bridge of the falls. I knew it was up to no good. If it had been helping someone the blue and red lights would be flashing, wouldn't they?"

"It was a police car," I shouted.

"Now, you've done it, Ellie. You made so much noise that they will know we are here and come to get us. I have to go now. I'm going now. You go home. You both leave now and go home. Maybe I will see you again. Maybe I will tell you more. But not now. It's too dangerous. Goodbye."

And before we could move, Josie was out the screen door and lost to sight, merging with the murky woods like a shadow passing.

"Darn it all, I can't keep my mouth shut," I said.

"You're right about that," Sarah agreed. "But I don't think Josie was mad, just worried about someone hearing us and coming after her. I think we could set up another meeting and she would tell us more, if you could be patient and keep quiet."

"I hope so. We came so close. We know it's a police car. It wouldn't be Dave, so it must be Colby. I knew something was going on with him and he has been searching for Josie. He must have killed Alice. Maybe now he wants to kill Josie. Oh my, I can't believe it. One of our own police."

"Now, don't go jumping to conclusions, Ellie. It might not have been a police vehicle. Maybe it was one of those hunters' SUV's with the spotlights on top. Or a patrol SUV from another town. Or maybe there had been a call and Colby was checking it out. We don't know anything yet. We have to talk to Josie again."

We trudged up the dirt road to the car. The wind was rising fast and branches were whipping, loose leaves flying and razor sharp drops of rain were zinging into our faces. I hoped we would make it to the car before the storm fully broke. Thunder boomed and then echoed off the sides of the mountains in a rolling boom, boom, and boom. Lightning started streaking the sky. At least the lightning allowed us to see where we were and how far we had to go to reach the car. After each stroke of lightning we were plunged into total darkness again. I had forgotten the flashlight and it sat with Sarah and my watches on Josie's railing.

Just as the clouds opened up and started dumping the rain, we made it to the car. We sat inside listening to the din of rain pelting the roof of the car. Water cascaded down the windows making visibility impossible.

"We might as well wait until this lets up a bit," I said. "I can't drive in this downpour."

"That's fine with me," Sarah said. "Well, we came so close to finding out who killed Alice and what really happened. That is, if Josie really did see what she says she did. What do you think, now? You've talked to her twice. Did she see Alice killed and the killer?"

"I still don't know," I said. "I can't get a grip on it in my mind, yet. She seems convinced of it, but why won't she just tell us so she can be helped? It's natural to want to relieve yourself when you hold a secret like that. She seems to want to hold the secret. Now why? Is it her mental condition, or is it to play up the drama, or is it just a story that she's making up as she goes along? Oh, I don't know."

We sat and listened to the rain and thunder and gasped at the lightning until the storm seemed to be abating. Weather is unpredictable in the mountains. Thunderstorms roar in and unload inches of rain and then roar on back out, heading east. Already the rain had changed to a fine mist and I hoped the clouds would lift so we could see the stars shining again. I started the car and turned toward home, driving slowly, avoiding the soft shoulders that were drenched and eroding into the road's culverts and dug ditches.

"The road crew will be busy tomorrow," Sarah said.

I was about to answer her when my headlights hit something ahead on the road. I slammed on the brakes, glad for the seat belt that held us in our seats.

"What's that?" I yelled.

There in front of us was a black bear, crossing the road.

Sarah and I said in unison, "It's a bear."

I continued, "Oh my god, make sure the windows are up."

Sarah whispered, "Put the windows down so we can see better."

The car windows went up and down and up and down again.

Sarah said, "Go forward slowly."

I slowly backed down the road. The bear just sat in the middle of the road staring at us.

Sarah said, "Oh, it's just a juvenile."

I said, "Look how big it is. Let's go another way."

Sarah said, "Go ahead slowly."

I managed to move the car forward a little, keeping my foot on the brake and my hand on the window buttons. Suddenly the bear stood up on its hind legs, its paws out in front of his huge body and stared at us as if daring us to keep coming.

Sarah said, "He's so beautiful." She was hanging out the passenger side window, trying to get a better view of the bear.

I said, "Oh my gosh. He's so big. He is going to attack us. He is in attack position. Close the windows."

Sarah said, "He's just a young bear being curious. He's standing up to see us better. Oh, look at his ears. They're wonderful."

I said, "Oh yeah? Roll up the windows if he comes any closer."

The bear got back on all fours and moved from the center of the road to the tall grass on the side.

Sarah said, "Move up closer now. Maybe we can see him better."

I said, "I'm driving straight by if you don't close your window." The windows went up and down and up and down again.

When we arrived at the spot where the bear had left the road we peered into the underbrush and high weeds. At first we didn't see anything. Then with a whoosh, and a spray of water, up came the bear on his hind feet again, closer to us this time.

Sarah said, "Look how glossy and beautiful he is. He's really checking us out. I haven't seen too many bears stand up like that."

I said, "He's getting ready to attack us now. He's really irritated that we are here. Put up the window. Get ready. What do we do if he attacks the car?"

Sarah said, "Ellie, don't be silly. He's just a baby."

I said, "He's not. He's taller than me when he stands up and weighs a whole lot more too. He could knock me flat."

Sarah said, "He's just a yearling. He's more scared of us than you are of him."

I said, "Oh no, I don't think so. I'm pretty scared. Don't you get out of this car. I don't even have a stick to save you if he grabs you."

Sarah said, "Don't worry, I won't. I don't want to scare him."

I said, "Scare Him! You would scare me. He scares me."

Just then the bear stooped down and disappeared into the meadow and we saw the grass moving as he entered the woods.

"Maybe he will come back, "I said. "Is he headed for my house?"

Sarah said, "I hope he comes back. It's so special to see a bear."

I said, "I hope not. Can he break the doors down?"

"I don't think so," said Sarah. "But I have heard of bears breaking into houses if they smell something good."

"Well, it's a good thing I ate up all that cherry pie before we set out," I said.

Now I had another worry to keep me up at night. Bears, murderers, and what next I wondered.

I dropped Sarah off at her car. We were both exhausted. I asked her to come in for tea, but she refused.

"I have to be at work at 7:00 to get the incoming mail," she said. "I think I have had quite enough for one night. I will talk to you tomorrow and we will work up plan number 2. Will you be all right here? Do you want to come home with me? You really don't have to worry about that bear. He's deep in the forest, trying to get away from us humans. And think of it this way. At least now you have your own bear story."

"Right," I said. "Everyone in town has at least one bear story. And now I have mine. I can't wait to tell it to everyone. Yes, I'll be all right. I'm going to pull all the shades down and close the curtains and lock the doors and put on the motion lights. I really wish I had a dog now."

"You'll be fine," Sarah laughed and drove off down the road. At least the bear had softened the shock of Alice's death for us. For a moment we were able to forget our pain and loss.

I ran to my house and scurried inside and barricaded the place as well as I could. I had enough excitement for one day and was ready for my bed. Butcher knives, bears, booms roared through my dreams all night, but they didn't keep me awake.

Chapter 11

WHEN I WOKE the next morning, the sadness of losing Alice hit me again and I had to drag myself out of bed. Even two cups of coffee didn't energize me and I sat on the screen porch and just stared out at the beautiful view in front of me with eyes blinded by tears. The overcast day seemed to join my mourning. Another day of rain seemed appropriate even though the high water in the rivers and brooks threatened to flood roads, cottages close to high water marks and even low built bridges at the bottom of the valley. Larry and the Hummingbird Falls road crew would have their hands full today.

The thought of the road crew brought me back to the reality of the tasks that lay ahead of me. I had been charged by Dave to help solve the mystery of Alice's death and I had volunteered to plan Alice's memorial service. Sarah and I still had to talk to Josie and find out what she knew. I didn't have time right now to sit and mourn the death of my friend. I had to get busy.

I called Chuck, the pastor of the Little Church in the village, and arranged a time for the service. We discussed a basic program that we would fill out more fully at the meeting we planned for this afternoon. Chuck was only too happy to help and knew the music and hymns that Alice loved the best. He would take charge of that part and would call the town horticulturalist, Heppie White, who did the flower arrangements for almost all of the occasions in town, from weddings to funerals. I only needed to call on other people to help set up the speakers, print up the finished program and plan the reception. Those tasks were enough to overwhelm me again and I sat back down and wept.

In time, I started to recover and called several people and actually made good progress. Mary was happy to be in charge of the reception and the food, relieved to have a way to help and do something for her good friend, Alice. She offered to call women from the church and ask them to prepare their favorite recipes and covered dishes. She knew the manager at the Inn across the road from the church and would check if she would provide reception space for free. She suggested that I call the Hummingbird Falls Weekly News, an eight page village paper which printed the selectman meeting news, local police record, church news, local little league scores, some ads and other tidbits of news, and ask them to donate the printed program.

The editor, John Staples, was glad to help. All I had to do was get the final program to him as soon as possible. He even offered to print a photograph of Alice on the front page. He said he was sure he had a good one of her in the news morgue. He would write the obituary as well, unless I knew someone else who wanted to do it. I assured him that he was the perfect one to write it and thanked him for the help.

Everything was coming together for the service and I began to feel a little better. At the town meeting tonight I could announce the time of the service and reach almost everyone that way. That would save a lot of phoning.

I spent the rest of the morning and most of the afternoon writing a eulogy for Alice. Working on finding the right words to express the essence of Alice helped me feel closer to her and helped with my sadness as well. I realized she would always be there with me in memory and that I could call her up in my mind any time I wished. That thought comforted me.

Finally it was time to head into town and meet with Chuck and then I would stop by the Post Office and talk with Sarah about how to approach Josie to find out what else she knew. Just before I left, the phone rang.

"Hello," I said.

"Hello, Mom? I'm so glad you're there. I really need to talk with you. I don't know what I'm going to do."

"Sandy, what's wrong? Are you all right? You didn't have an accident, did you? That traffic down there in Florida is so awful."

"Mom, it isn't the traffic. It's Marilyn."

"Marilyn? Was she in an accident? Oh no. Is she hurt?"

"Mom, no. Marilyn wasn't in an accident. Just let me tell you. You listen, OK?"

"OK. Marilyn is all right and you are, too. So, anything else shouldn't be too bad. Tell me."

"I don't know how to say it. I'm... Marilyn's... Marilyn and I are talking about a separation, maybe a divorce."

"No, Sandy. Not you and Marilyn. You love each other so much. What's happened? Did she do something foolish? Did you?"

"No, Mom. We have just been fighting for months and we're so tired of it. Every time we try to just be together we end up in a fight. So, we decided to call it quits. Life is too short to fight everyday about not washing my cereal dish or whose turn it is to turn the sprinkler on."

I didn't know what to say. Sandy had fallen in love with Marilyn while he was in his senior year at Florida State. When I met her at their graduation, I fell in love with her too. After a few years of living together in a tiny apartment while they found jobs and started their careers, they married. That was only two years ago. Both had good jobs and shared their together time on their little Grady boat, fishing and cruising the Florida coast and intercoastal water way. The last time I saw them, in February during school vacation on my annual get away, they seemed very happy and were talking about starting a family. Something had gone wrong in the last few months.

"Sandy, what are you really fighting about? Do you know?"

There was silence on the other end of the phone.

"Sandy? Are you there?"

"Yeah, Mom. I'm here. We seem to fight about every little thing. But what we're mostly fighting over is having a baby."

"Are you having a baby, Sandy? Oh my god. You can't break up now if you're having a baby."

"Hold on, Mom. We aren't having a baby. We are fighting about having a baby."

"Oh," I said.

"I'm not sure I am ready for that step yet. Marilyn is. She says if I loved her enough, I would want to have a family with her. I do, I want that, but not now. We've only been married two years. I'm not even used to that yet. What should I do? Help me, Mom. I don't want to lose Marilyn, but I can't go ahead with something I don't feel ready for either. That would be a real mess. I'm afraid I might feel resentful toward Marilyn or the baby. That would be awful for all of us."

"Oh Sandy. I am so sorry. What a terrible dilemma. How can I help? Do you want me to talk with Marilyn?"

"No, no, don't do that. I don't want her to know I told you. She would go ballistic if she found out I was telling you about our private matters before she was ready to tell you herself. I just need some advice from you. What would you do?"

"First, let me say how much I love you and Marilyn and I know, I can tell how much you mean to each other. You don't want to jeopardize the wonderful love you have for each other. So, I wouldn't do anything until I got some help," I said. "Find a good therapist, someone who works with couples and has experience with this problem. It's a common one. A lot of couples go through this, so you're not alone. Give the therapy a good chance to work, at least six months before you make any decision. That's what I would do."

"That's a good idea, Mom. I think Marilyn would go along with that, even though she's a very private person and likes to keep her business to herself. I'll ask my friend Toby about a therapist. Do you remember meeting him? He's a counselor here in town. He probably knows someone good to go to. Then I'll bring it up to Marilyn.

"Thanks, Mom. I knew I could count on you. You're always there when I need you."

"Thanks, honey, for the kind words. Of course, I would do anything I could to help you and Marilyn. Call me anytime you want to talk. One other thing. If I were you I might tell Marilyn that you talked with me. There shouldn't be any secrets. Then maybe she'll feel she can talk with me too. I would love to talk with her about this. Please tell her so, will you?"

"I'll think about that, Mom. Thanks again. I'm going to call Toby right now. Take care. You are fine, aren't you? Nothing ever happens up in those back woods you love so much."

"No, dear, nothing much ever happens up here. I am just fine. Let me hear from you soon, all right? I love you."

"I love you, too, bye."

I shook my head as I hung up the phone. Sandy sounded pretty distraught. Now I had something more to worry about. I loved Sandy and Marilyn so much and wanted the best for them. I hoped they could save their marriage. I felt far away and helpless, but reminded myself that my children are grown adults and can take care of their lives without me. I felt glad that I was the kind of mom whose kids would call when they needed some help. Christopher and I had raised the children the best we knew how, no easy job, especially after Chris was diagnosed with prostate cancer, suffered through surgeries, chemotherapy and radiation, and then died. I could only trust that our parenting had provided them with the coping skills and values that would ease them on their journeys through the struggles of life.

But, I had things to take care of in my life, too. So I picked up my car keys and started on my way down to town. I could hear the waters roaring again. The creeks, filled by last night's downpour, were filling the rivers to capacity. As I drove toward the Coldwater River, I noticed the Falls Road was open again and so I drove that route into town. I stopped several times by the side of the falls to watch the furious water crashing downstream, leaping boulders and smashing over the shoreline, which was usually dry land. The waters were white with foam and angry looking. The falls were scary, threatening looking. No one was in the water, of course. It would be too dangerous with the current so strong. I didn't see any hummingbirds around and even the tourists had more sense than to hang out around the falls. They were probably spending the day at the outlet store malls or antique and souvenir shopping in the large town of Greenberg. I'm sure the inns were experiencing the summer horror of cancellations because of the weather. In a town supported by summer tourist dollars, bad weather meant hard times. Moreover, with additional rain forecast, flooding was a real possibility. That meant that the lower bridge, even the village, could be in trouble. We would probably find out more about that at the meeting tonight, too.

I drove to the Little Church in the village. Built in 1845, the church was typical New England architecture, a simple rectangle with tall windows, and a two-story roofline with a small steeple. Hostas lined the flag stone walk up to the unpainted oak front door. As I stepped into the front entryway, my eyes slowly adjusted to the dim interior. I walked down the aisle toward Pastor Chuck's office which was to the right of the altar. Suddenly, I stopped. To the left, next to the wall, a woman huddled, head bowed and body shaking with sobs.

It was Pauline. I slid down the pew toward her. "Pauline, are you all right?" I asked quietly.

She jerked her head up, startled by my voice. "I didn't see you there, Ellie," she said. She hastily wiped her eyes and blew her nose with a tissue.

"Can I help?" I asked. "Tell me what the matter is."

"I can't," she sobbed. "I can't talk about it." She bent over and sobbed even harder. I put my arm around her and whispered comforting words, wondering what had happened to make her so upset.

Gradually her sobbing slowed and she murmured so low I could hardly hear her, "It is all my fault that she is dead. I can't talk about it. If it weren't for me she would be alive now. How could I have done it? I was just trying to help and it all went wrong." She broke down in tears again.

I let her cry for a few more minutes and patted her hand. "Pauline, who are you talking about? What did you do?"

"It was for Colby. I just wanted him to be happy. He has had such a terrible life. Abandoned by his mother right after he was born. Rejected as a baby by his adoptive parents and then foster home after foster home. No wonder he acted out. Finally, the only place he had to go was the farm for emotionally troubled boys. That's where he met Dave. Dave was his big brother and if it weren't for Dave, I don't know what would have happened to Colby."

She paused to wipe at her tears and blow her nose.

"By the time I met Colby, Dave had arranged for him to come to the Regional High School for this area and Colby took to sports and turned his life around. We became great friends and then we went steady. Then everything went wrong."

Pauline dissolved into tears again. I sat close to her and patted her arm to show my support. I was confused by her rambling story. First, she was talking about taking the blame for someone's death and then she was talking about Colby's history.

"Everything might have worked out if only Colby could have stopped trying to find his mother. He just couldn't let it go. I never should have helped him. Now look at what's happened." Pauline hugged herself and bent her head down onto her chest.

"Pauline," I said, "I'm confused and I am not following what you are telling me. Who would be alive? What have you done?"

Just then, Pastor Chuck stuck his head out of his office door. "I thought I heard voices out here. Hi Ellie. I'm ready for you. Hi there, Pauline. Getting some quiet time?"

Pauline quickly raised her head and tried to smile. "Yes," Pauline answered. "It was slow next door at the library so I came in here to take a break. I have to get back now." She gathered up her things and rushed up the aisle and out the door.

I stood up and walked to Chuck's office. I decided not to mention what Pauline had told me. If she had wanted Chuck to know I figured she would have told him herself. But I was shaken to the core.

It sounded like Pauline and maybe Colby had been involved in someone's death. Maybe they were involved with Alice's death in some way. I knew I would have to talk to Dave as soon as I could.

Chapter 12

CHUCK AND I worked on the program for Alice's memorial service. Chuck had already chosen Alice's favorite hymns and several readings. The organist and soloist had been notified and would be rehearsing tomorrow. The floral arrangements were ordered and would be delivered before the service. When we finalized the program, Chuck suggested that I go right over to the News office to start the printing process. I thanked Chuck for his help and said I would get back to him and left for the newspaper office.

John greeted me at the door. "I found a great picture of Alice in the files. It will look fine on the front of the program. I also have a poem that she published in the News a few weeks ago. I think that would be appropriate for the back cover. Here, take a look. You probably remember reading it."

Finding Faith

Every day I watch the progress of
The green pointy shoots of daffodil stems
As they drill through the stiff spring earth
On their journey to beauty.

One day, enclosed green bumps break into

Blooms spectacular with yellow green petals
And I lose myself in their glory.

I breathe in the flashy flower.
High with the gaudy aroma,
Dazed by the brilliant color,
I trip on the conspicuous splendor,
As if what I see, the visible, is the only reality.

Indiscernible, the brown, dirt covered bulb
Pumps strength for the growth,
Grounds the jade spike as it flares into golden flower
And crafts the yellow beauty into a charmer
That attracts adoration for its season of its being.

Too soon the lemon shade fades and the stem browns.
Wilted, the venerated fresh beauty of yesterday
Dies away, withered, ugly and decayed.
I try to remember that when the daffodil disappears
It lives transformed, unseen,
Waiting for its moment which will come again
When it is time.

But I am not consoled today.
I turn to the tulips and lilacs,
Just beginning to show their tint
Amidst their leaves of green.
As I revel in their beautiful birth,
I grapple with their predictable demise,
And faith's tiny roots take hold in my heart.

I broke down into sobs. John's eyes were filled with tears as well. When I could talk again I said, "This is so like Alice. The poem is just right for the program. Thank you so much, John, for remembering it."

John offered me a tissue and dabbed at his eyes with another one.

"When do you want the program completed?"

"As soon as you can, John. The funeral will be in three days, as the date on the program indicates. I really appreciate your help. Alice has a lot of friends in this town."

"That's for sure, Ellie. I don't know anyone who wouldn't want to help. I'll have the obituary finished and ready for tomorrow's edition of the paper. I'm going to feature Alice's life and the history of her family in Hummingbird Falls on the front page. We can memorialize her life in print that way and let everyone know the time for the service and reception. Anything else you need my help with?"

I gave John a hug. "Not that I can think of right now, John. Oh, yes. You have been printing this paper for how many years now?"

"Over thirty years, if you can believe it. Why?"

"John, you have been the hub of the comings and goings of this town for so long. If Alice was murdered, do you have any guesses who might have killed her?"

John scratched his head and looked down at the floor. "I have been obsessing over who might have killed her, Ellie. I guess everyone is. We all look at each other a little differently now, I think, wondering could it be him? Could it be her? Will she be next? Will the killer strike again?"

"I know. But do you think of anyone especially?"

John looked at me. "Of course. I think of James, her brother. It was too much of a coincidence him showing up and then Alice dying. I think of Josie. Although she is usually fearful and gentle, I have seen her go into murderous rages when she is off her meds or someone tries to get her to the doctor or hospital. She could have killed Alice. And then there is…"

John paused. "Lots of gossip and small town rumors run around here, Ellie. Usually not worth the breath to repeat and most of them false. But I have heard some whisperings about Colby visiting Alice. Some say Pauline, and maybe Mike Greeley, were pretty upset about that. Pauline, Colby and James go way back, you know. They all graduated from the Regional School in the same class, some thirteen years ago. They knew Alice, of course, but she was much older than them, same age as Mike, and never really had anything to do with them because she was away at school. Even though James was her half brother, she was almost old enough to be his mother. Other than that, I've heard that some folks think the Wilson murderer has come back. Since the Wilson's' murder is the only other homicide that has occurred in Hummingbird Falls, I guess it's natural to try to make a connection. But that seems pretty unlikely to me."

"Anyone else?" I asked.

"Well, this is pretty far fetched, but Margaret has had some run-ins with Alice over the years. Mostly about conservation issues, zone restrictions, limiting retail stores downtown. Margaret has been heard saying that if Alice wasn't here, the town would be much more prosperous and her gallery would be doing a better business."

"But, Margaret? She's one of Alice's best friends, I thought. We meet together all the time. She wouldn't ever do anything to hurt Alice, would she? I've never heard her say anything against Alice personally."

John smiled. "I've come to believe that old cliché, Ellie, that you can't tell a book by its cover and that what someone seems to be is often pretense, and could be very different from what lurks within. Ever seen those ruby throated hummingbirds? Beautiful to look at but aggressive as hell against anything that gets in its way. Margaret's like that, I think. She looks great, sounds great, but is tenacious about getting what she wants."

John added, "My other suspicions? Anyone who was in this town that night."

I thanked John for his help and left, my head reeling with what I had learned. I would just have to process it later when I had more time.

My next stop was the post office. I wanted to arrange a time to talk with Sarah about our next meeting with Josie. But, Sarah had a long line waiting for service, so I just waved at her, got my mail out of my mailbox and headed out. I flipped through the mail and was pleased to see a letter from my daughter among the bills and junk mail. I looked forward to reading it when I got home. But first I had to talk with Dave about what I had discovered from John and more importantly, about what Pauline had told me in the church. Maybe he would know what she was talking about.

When I arrived at the police station the only one around was Betsy, the dispatcher. She said both Dave and Colby were out on calls and asked me if I wanted to leave a message. I said no, I would check in later. I headed for the pastry shop. I had only about an hour to kill before tonight's meeting, so instead of heading back up the mountain, I would just wait there and maybe read my daughter's letter over a blueberry turnover and hazelnut coffee.

The pastry shop was almost empty. Besides a couple of older men having coffee in the back booth, the only person there was Colby, sitting alone, head down, nursing his coffee. He looked up as I came in and motioned for me to join him. I felt awkward instantly. Not only had Pauline just revealed more that I ever expected to know about Colby, but I had also reported Colby's inappropriate behavior to Dave who would have spoken to him by now about my complaints. I was nervous about his reaction. But, knowing I couldn't avoid him in this small town and had to face him sometime, I walked over and sat down.

"Hi, Colby," I said. Then I noticed the tears in his eyes. "Are you all right?"

"Not really, Ellie. I'm feeling kind of bad right now. Sorry. It's just that I never expected that we would lose Alice. I mean, I just got to know her a little and now she's gone. I can't believe it. I liked her a lot. She cared about me."

I didn't know what to say. Colby's sadness over Alice's death surprised me. I didn't know about their connection other than from the gossip I had heard.

I ventured, "I'm sorry, too, Colby. The whole town is sorry. Were you and Alice especially close?"

He looked down into his coffee. "We just began to learn about each other and that felt very good to both of us. We both were without families and that drew us close together, I think. She didn't have an easy life even though she had plenty of money. My life hasn't been so great either. She was a great woman."

A tear slipped down one cheek and Colby hurriedly wiped it off. He shook his head as if to get rid of his thoughts.

"Speaking of sorry," Colby said. "I want to tell you how sorry I am about how I talked to you. I want to apologize. Dave told me you were upset with me. I guess I went overboard. I'm sorry. Sometimes I try too hard to get women to like me. I don't mean anything by it. I just try to be friendly, but somehow it goes further than I realize. Will you accept my apology? It won't happen again, I promise you. I am really sorry."

He sounded so sincere. His blue eyes were pleading with me and there was no sound of sarcasm in his voice, nor did his face register anything but openness and grief. I decided to forgive him this time, especially now that I knew about his traumatic past and his feelings for Alice. But I knew I would still be very careful around him, no matter how sorry he seemed.

"Colby, thank you for apologizing. I forgive you and I just hope it won't happen again. I didn't expect you to talk to me that way and it worried me. That's why I spoke to Dave about it. But now it's taken care of, so let's put it behind us and move on."

"Thanks, Ellie. I feel better now and I hope you do too." He took a drink of his coffee. "By the way, have you seen Josie today? I am still looking for her. I stopped down there yesterday and thought I heard something, but I didn't see her. She is a hard one to find if she doesn't want to be found."

"Uh, no, I haven't seen her today. But Sarah and I did stop by last night to deliver her mail and she was all right. Just the usual paranoia and worrying that she engages in. So, I think you can cross her off your list. Anyway, unfortunately we know Alice is the one who was found in the falls, so you don't need to continue your worrying about Josie."

To change the subject I said, "Oh Colby, I have a bear story now. I knew I couldn't really belong in this town until I had a bear story like everyone else and now I have one. When we were coming back from Josie's last night we saw a huge black bear on the Durkin Farm Road, right in the middle of the road. I have never seen a bear in the wild before and my adrenaline was pumping pretty fast. All I could think about was that old Stephen King movie, *Cujo*. I remembered hearing of a bear in the area that had broken into a house through the locked windows and screens when no one was home and then trashed the house."

"You're right, Ellie. We've had quite a few bear complaints this year. When I was out at Josie's house yesterday morning, I thought I heard a bear. I had my gun ready; you can count on that. But, you know, Ellie, you can't believe all the bear stories you hear. Some are pretty exaggerated."

"That's probably true, Colby. But I'm telling you my story just like it happened".

I loved telling stories, even if I did change them a little bit to make myself look less foolish and a lot more courageous than I had been last night. I decided embellishment just made my tale more interesting.

When I finished Colby said, "Ellie, that's a beautiful story and I'm glad you got to see your first bear. You fit in here so well. You appreciate our environment like we do. We know the wildlife is special and what helps to make Hummingbird Falls the wonderful place it is. That's why so many of us are against the selling of the old farms, like Mike Greeley is doing. The condos come in and the animals move out or get killed as nuisances. I lived on a farm once and I learned that nature is soothing and healing. It helped bring me back into myself when I was having a hard time. It still helps me to go out into the country and just walk the trails, see the animal signs, hear the birds and marvel in the beauty of everything around us. I come back refreshed, a better person. So congratulations. You will have to come into the pastry shop when it's busy and announce you saw a bear and want to tell your story. And you're a brave woman. Most people would freak out if they saw a bear. You didn't. But don't go overboard. When we get a bear call we get our guns out just in case. There are rogue bears just like there are bad people."

I looked at Colby. I was seeing him in a different way now. My nervousness had disappeared. "Sarah helped me stay calm, a little, I have to admit. And time to think over the experience probably has changed the memory some from the way I really reacted. Later reflection is sometimes a better story than first reaction, don't you think?" I was feeling a bit guilty about not quite telling Colby the whole truth about the way I handled the bear situation.

"Anyway," Colby said, "To digress a little, I do need to talk to Josie. I want to be sure she's not making up stories that will scare people or lead them to think things that aren't true."

"What stories is she telling?"

"I'm not exactly sure. But every time something happens in Hummingbird Falls, she makes a big fuss about it and spreads all kinds of nonsense around. I don't want Alice's case contaminated by Josie's tales."

"Has the Medical Examiner reported the findings yet?" I asked.

"Yes, but Dave is keeping the report to himself to study before tonight's meeting. He hasn't even told me what the results are. I think that's a little strange, after all I am his assistant. But he said I would find out when everyone else does."

The door to the pastry shop opened. A thin man with glasses carrying a brief case walked over to our booth. He looked at Colby's uniform.

"Officer, perhaps you can help me. I am looking for Ms. Eleanor Hastings, who lives here in Hummingbird Falls. Do you know where I can find her? Her address is 1201 Durkin Farm Road."

"Well, I sure can help you with that, sir." Colby said with a smile. "She's sitting right here."

The man looked at me. "You are Eleanor Hastings?"

"Yes," I answered. "And you are?"

"I am Samuel Compton. I am Alice Foster's lawyer. I need to speak to you in private."

"What about?" I asked.

Colby stood up. "I'll just get moving along. I have some things to do before the meeting tonight. See you there, Ellie. Mr. Compton, excuse me."

Mr. Compton took Colby's place at the table. "Were you aware that you are the executrix of Alice Foster's will?" he asked.

I gasped. "No, I had no idea. Are you sure? Why did she name me the executrix?"

"She told me that her only living relatives were not appropriate. She is estranged from her half-brother and, well, other blood relatives have been named in the will, but are not recognized legally, at this point, anyway. She said you were a fair and honest friend who could be trusted to carry out her wishes. Do you have any objections?"

"No, I don't think so. I'm just shocked. I was executrix for my husband's will and am familiar with the probate process. I never expected to be in this position, though. I am honored she chose me when she has so many other lifetime friends here in the village."

"I think that was one of the reasons she chose you, Ms. Hastings. If she chose one of them, then the others might have felt slighted. You being an outsider of sorts, although a good friend, eliminates the pressure on everyone else of either being chosen or not being chosen."

"I think I understand that. Alice wouldn't have wanted anyone from Hummingbird Falls to be upset or feel left out. She is a wise woman. How do I get started, Mr. Compton?"

"Can you meet with me tomorrow at 1:00 pm at my office in Greenberg? I can go over the will with you and then we can plan a time for the reading of the will for the beneficiaries. Until then, I would keep this between you and me. No sense in stirring everything up before we are ready to reveal the contents of the will. Of course, as you probably know, you are also one of the beneficiaries."

"I didn't know that," I said. "What do you mean? Alice left me something?"

"Oh yes, indeed. I thought you knew. You will be quite surprised then. Let's leave it for now. I will explain everything to you tomorrow. Good day, Ms. Hastings."

He left me sitting with my mouth open. Dear Alice. Not only had she named me executrix of her will, she had also left me something. What could it be? And what did it mean?

Chapter 13

I DIDN'T REALLY have much time to think about Alice's will because the meeting was scheduled to begin in just a half an hour and I wanted to see Sarah before the meeting started. Townspeople were rushing into the pastry shop to buy coffee and snacks to take to the school cafeteria where the meeting was being held. I said hello to several people I knew and wondered what they would think when they found out that I was to be executrix of the will of their friend and neighbor, Alice Foster. I felt a heavy responsibility and deep anxiety. What was I getting myself into? Or rather, what had Alice got me into?

I drove over to Sarah's house and was relieved to find her car in the driveway.

She answered my knock. "I was just grabbing a bite to eat before going to the meeting. I have plenty. Want some salad with grilled chicken?"

I never could say no to food. "Sure, that would be great. I have been so busy I've only had coffee. Well, a blueberry turnover, too, but it was a small one."

We ate quickly and quietly. While I was washing the dishes, Sarah asked, "Have you figured out what to do about Josie?"

I said, "Not really. I suppose we could go up to her place after the meeting and try to talk to her again. What do you think?"

"Depends on when the meeting gets over. If it is short, then we could visit her tonight. If it goes on forever, like most meetings, we had better plan on tomorrow."

"Fine with me. We had better leave now, though. I want to get a seat up front where I can hear what everyone is saying."

We hurried to our cars and drove to the school. The parking lot was already almost full. Lights blazed through the cafeteria windows and we could see that the tables were filling up fast. We joined the crowd headed for the doors, nodding at some people and saying hello to others.

At precisely 7:30 Dave stood and faced the crowd. I didn't see Colby anywhere. Perhaps he was directing traffic outside. Pauline was missing as well. Most of the faces in the audience were ones I recognized, but a few were strangers. A group around one table, keeping to themselves, was obviously from the art community up the hill. Their hippie type clothes and ingenious hair colors, piercings, and tattoos identified them clearly. Margaret was sitting with them. I gave her a wave and John's words ran through my mind like a fire through dry grass. I looked at her closely. She looked fabulous, all done up in a red satin turban and long flowing silk dress. Her dangling earrings reflected silver sparkles as she tossed her head. Could she have killed Alice? I stamped out these thoughts and made myself continue to look around the room. A well dressed man came in the door and stood by himself against the sidewall. He looked brooding, yet somewhat familiar. I thought he could be Alice's brother; the coloring and shape of his nose and eyes resembled hers. Other folks sitting at the tables looked like hard working outdoors types, tanned and lined faces, John Deere caps firmly on their heads, hands rough and chapped. Foresters, farmers, saw mill workers, country people all drawn to town to hear news of one of their own. John sat with a group of business men and their wives. I nodded to those who smiled or recognized me and then turned to Sarah.

"Does anyone here look suspicious to you?"

"What a silly question, Ellie. Everyone looks suspicious to me. I'm just glad Josie isn't here. That would really raise the roof."

"Do you think she might show up?" I asked.

"You can never be sure about Josie," she answered.

Just then Dave cleared his throat and called the room to attention. "As you all know, we are here because of the death of Alice Foster. Her body was found at the bottom of the falls two days ago. Most of us knew Alice and loved her. She was one of us, her folks were part of our community and her grandparents and great-grandparents helped to settle Hummingbird Falls long ago. We will miss her. Now, Ellie Hastings has an announcement to make and then I will get on to the business of tonight."

I was surprised to be named and then I remembered that I was to let everyone know about the plans for Alice's funeral service.

I stood and said, "I am so sorry about the passing of our friend Alice. Several of us have spoken together and planned a memorial service to be held on Sunday at the Little Church in the Village at 10:30. Anyone who wishes to speak about Alice, say something about his or her connection to her or tell a remembrance will have a chance during the service. So I hope you will all come to celebrate her life. Afterwards, there will be refreshments at the Inn across the street. Everyone is invited, so please come. We welcome donations of food for the reception. Please contact Mary Shaffer who is in charge of the food. Thank you. Oh, please don't send flowers. Instead, a donation in Alice's name to the Historical Society, the Garden Club or the Environmental Association would be appreciated. And be sure to read a copy of the Hummingbird News tomorrow for more information and a wonderful story on Alice's life."

I sat down, glad to be out of the center of attention. Dave stood up again.

"I'll get right to it. I received the preliminary report from the Medical Examiner for the State just a few hours ago. They performed an autopsy and did other tests to determine the cause of Alice's death. Not all the tests are back yet. Some won't be finished for 6-8 weeks.

But the Medical Examiner believes she can say that the death was not accidental." Dave paused to let the whispered talking rise and then fall before he went on.

"It seems that she was killed before she went into the water." Again the voices rose as people exchanged their thoughts.

"It appears she was thrown from the Iron Bridge at the top of the falls after she died. The injuries to her body and head after death were caused by the trauma of hitting the stones after going over the bridge at a height of 35 feet and from being swept down the falls and hitting the boulders on the way. When she was found by Bobby Brady at 7:30 am, she had been dead approximately seven to ten hours, putting the time of her death Monday night, sometime after 9:30 pm and before 12:30."

"What killed her?" a voice called out.

"I was getting to that," Dave said. "At this point, we are not certain. Alice sustained many fractures of her skull, most from her head hitting the rocks in the falls. The Medical Examiner thinks one of the blows to her head, the fatal one, was caused by another source. I am unable to speak about it now, as we need more information as to what that source was. But at this point, we are calling Alice's death a homicide. And we are asking that anyone who knows anything about what happened to Alice to come forward and talk to us. In addition, anyone who talked to, or saw Alice in the three days prior to her death, I want to talk to after the meeting."

Again, a babble of voices interrupted Dave. "Does anyone have any questions before I go on?"

A woman called out, "Are you saying that Alice was murdered? Is there a murderer running around Hummingbird Falls?"

Dave answered, "Unfortunately, yes. Someone killed Alice and dumped her body into the falls. Yes, we have a murderer out there. We don't know that the killer is from Hummingbird Falls. That's one thing we will be working on and you can help us with. If you saw a stranger, or an unknown vehicle, or anything unusual let me know. I understand that most tourists fit that description, but we have to check them all out, too. Anyone, at this point, could be the killer. They could be still here, or they could have left. We don't know."

Another voice called out, "Is the State helping or are just you and Colby investigating?"

"For now, it is just my office that is in charge of the investigation. Of course, the State has been here and done the forensics and the Medical Examiner will continue her own research as to causes. If we need more help, we can call on the State at any time. I may have to do that."

"Does this murder have anything to do with the Wilson massacre?"

Dave flinched. "I don't believe so. But we will be checking on that as well. As you know, the Wilson case remains open. The killer was never found. It would seem very unlikely that this murder was committed by the same person, but we aren't ruling it out."

"Why was Alice killed? Was her house robbed?"

"There is no sign of breaking or entering. James, Alice's brother, hasn't noticed anything missing. So we have ruled out motive of robbery."

People stared at the man leaning against the wall and his face reddened as he drew their attention. I guessed right. That must be James Foster.

"But why was she killed?" another voice called out.

"We don't know that yet. We are looking into it. Don't worry. We will find out why and who and we will be working on solving this homicide as soon as possible. Now, any more questions?"

"I got a question." A small thin man, with a snide look on his face, stood up. "What makes you think you can solve this murder when you couldn't do nothing about my brother, his wife and kid? You never found their killer. You most likely won't. Haven't heard anything about the Wilson case in a long time."

Dave took some time to answer. Then he said, "I'm so very sorry about your brother and his family. I have not forgotten about them and I will never forget about them. Their case will remain open until the person responsible for their deaths is brought to justice. I learned a lot investigating that case and in the years since then. I feel confident that I can find who killed Alice Foster. Be patient with me please. I will do my best for you, for her, for us all."

There was mild applause in support of Dave. As it settled down he added. "I want to talk to everyone who saw or talked to Alice in the three days prior to her death. Please stand if you fit in that category."

Everyone looked around. Slowly people began to stand. James Foster took a step forward. Mike Greeley stood. Colby raised his hand from where he was standing in the back of the room. Next to him, Pauline raised her hand too. Margaret stood up. Others stood or raised their hands. In all, there were eleven people.

"One other matter before we close. The rain's creating quite a problem out there. The rivers are at their highest point in years and the ditches on the sides of the roads are very soft. You need to be careful driving. If we get more heavy rain there is danger of flooding. Please keep your radios tuned in. We may have to close some of the roads and possibly some of the bridges if the water gets too high. Now, I am going to call this meeting closed, except for those of you who identified yourselves as having contact with Alice or knowing something about her death. Thanks to you all. If you have any information, no matter how insignificant it may seem, please contact me. The meeting is adjourned."

But before anyone could move a scream curdled the air. A whirling rag covered form ran into the cafeteria. Everyone panicked and many ducked under the tables and covered their heads. Others just stood froozen, shocked into slience.

"She is dead, killed, murdered and drowned. She is gone. She didn't need to be, but she is. No one else should die. You must stop it now," the figure screamed.

It had to be Josie, although her head was completely covered and her body disguised by layers of tattered clothes.

People began to peek out from under the tables. Dave started to walk toward the figure.

"Josie," Dave said. "Please calm down. We will be glad to listen to you."

The closer Dave walked to her, the further Josie backed off. "Don't come near me," she screeched. "I saw Alice alive. I saw her dead. I know what happened. It isn't fair. She was always nice to me. Didn't treat me like some of you." She whirled around pointing at different people.

"You probably think I killed her. But I didn't. But I will tell you who did."

Suddenly Colby yelled out from behind Josie, "I've got her." As he ran to grab her, Josie whooped and darted down between the tables and disappeared out the side door of the cafeteria. A mass of people tried to follow her out, crowding the area and blocking Dave from reaching the door. Colby ran out the front door, intending to circle the building until he reached the side door. But when he arrived, Josie was long gone into the woods. Townspeople stood around at the edges of the forest looking halfheartedly for the escaped woman.

Dave caught Colby's arm. "What the hell did you do that for?"

"I'm sorry, boss. Really. I thought I would just grab her before she got away and then we could take her to the office and hear what she has to say. I thought we should hear it before she blabbed out some nonsense that everyone would hear and go crazy about. I didn't know she could move so fast."

"Well, get the SUV and find her. I'll take my vehicle and look as well. She probably won't go home, knowing we are looking for her, but check there in case. I am going to find Mike and ask him to bring his bloodhounds down here to trace her. You get on the road. And if you do find her, call. Don't try to stop her or touch her. She will just freak out again. Now get going."

Colby ran for the SUV and flicked on the flashing red and blue lights and tore out of the school parking lot.

People stood and merged into clusters, talking and gesturing. Slowly they made their way out of the cafeteria and stood in groups in the parking lot, discussing what they had learned, what they thought they knew, and expressing their unease about the safety of Hummingbird Falls. Josie's behavior and disclosure was in everyone's conversation, ratcheting the anxiety lever too high. The mood was as dark as the sky, which was clouded with huge black thunderheads. Thick drops of rain started to fall, driving everyone to the protection of their cars. The meeting was over.

Chapter 14

SARAH AND I headed for our cars. "I think we should go right up to Josie's, don't you?" I asked. Sarah hesitated. She looked around at the parking lot which was emptying out.

"I don't know. I don't think so. Not after what happened tonight. She won't go home. She'll be too scared."

"But it's going to be raining so hard. Won't she need shelter? And she's very upset. Maybe she needs help. We should at least try to see if she's there. We agreed to plan 2, Sarah. We have to find out what Josie knows. It's clear now that she really wants to tell what she saw. She came all the way to the meeting to let everyone know who killed Alice. We need to talk to her. What 's the matter with you?"

"Let the police take care of it. They're looking for her and will probably find her. They'll take her to the police station and interview her. Dave will find out what she knows. I have a lot to do. I haven't slept well. I really don't feel like going all the way up there tonight." Sarah looked at the car keys she was holding. She looked at a car that was backing out. She seemed to look everywhere but at me. Her mood had changed completely.

"Are you all right, Sarah?"

"Yes," she snapped. "Stop asking me that. We will just be wasting our time trying to get Josie to talk. And then, if she does talk, it will probably be delusional and nothing but her fantasies. I think we should just drop the whole thing. Go talk to Dave if you want. Ask him to go up to Josie's with you. I don't know why I got involved with this in the first place. It's just too much for me."

"Sarah, what has made you change your mind all of a sudden? You were certainly ready to visit Josie again when we talked before the meeting."

"I know. But the meeting tonight was so terrible. It's all too sad. Alice is dead. Josie's so sick. I didn't sleep last night. That Wilson murder. It's pouring again and I don't want to walk down that dark road to Josie's house. If the murderer was at the meeting tonight, Josie's in terrible danger. I don't want to be anywhere near cold blooded killers or their victims."

"If you come with me, just this one more time, then I won't bother you anymore. I can't go by myself because Josie's irritated with me. And Josie responds to you. She trusts you more than anyone else, I think. At least I got that impression from the way she reacted to you last night. Just come with me tonight and then I won't ask any more of you. I promise. We can drive up the road. We won't walk. That will make it easier and take less time. Please Sarah."

She hesitated. "I don't want to, I really don't. I have a bad feeling about this whole thing. But I will go with you, just because I said I would. But it's the last time. I'm getting out of this investigation. It isn't any fun anymore. It's just plain spooky."

"I know," I said. "Thank you for sticking with me through tonight. We'll get her to tell us who killed Alice. We will do this for our friend Alice. You talk and I'll keep my mouth shut. I promise. Meet me at my house and we will drive in my car. I hope she's home and willing to cooperate."

Sarah answered, "Maybe after what she has been through tonight she'll talk to us. At least she knows Dave knows that Alice is dead, and that she was murdered. Those two facts are real. So, Josie's story has been verified and when she names the murderer she has a better chance of being believed. We only have to convince her to tell us who did it. Isn't it strange that Josie has become the key to solving Alice's murder?"

We drove off. Sarah followed me up the hill. I wondered what was really bothering her and why she had changed her mind so suddenly about investigating the crime with me. I felt let down and somewhat perplexed. I felt like I was missing something and I didn't know what. But, I was hoping that tonight would answer the biggest questions of all. Who killed Alice and why.

Chapter 15

WE DROPPED OFF Sarah's car at my cottage and drove together up to Josie's road. Neither one of us said anything. We listened as the windshield wipers fought the sheets of rain trying to obscure our vision. We were buried in our own thoughts and concerns. We bumped down Josie's road, trying to avoid the huge puddles that had filled in the ruts. At places the road turned into a pond and the water slapped at my fenders. The road was close to impassable, but jolting along in the car beat walking blindly down that dark road and getting soaked stumbling through the pools of muddy water.

The house was as dark as it had been last night. We pulled to a stop at the front porch and climbed the steps. We reclaimed out watches and I picked up my little flashlight and turned it on. We knocked on the door. No answer. We knocked repeatedly and called out quietly,

"Josie, it is Sarah and Ellie. Are you there?" Complete silence; no one answered.

"What should we do?" Sarah asked me.

"Let's try the door." It was locked.

"Let's try around back," I said.

Sarah said, "I don't want to do that. Let's go back to the car."

"Come on, Sarah. We've come all the way up here. I'm going to go around back."

Holding the flashlight I led the way around the side of Josie's house to the back screen porch. Sarah stumbled after me. I tried the door. It was unlocked.

"Shall we go in?" I asked.

"No," Sarah answered. "We've done enough. I want to go back."

I called out, "Josie, are you there? It is just Sarah and Ellie. We want to talk to you. Please let us in."

No response. Only the rain beating on our heads and dinging off Josie's tin roof broke the silence.

"I'll just knock on the back door. Maybe she didn't want to open the front door. And if she doesn't answer then we'll go. Okay?"

I stepped in the screen door to the porch, lighting the floor so I wouldn't trip over anything. And then I stopped so quickly that Sarah bumped into me.

"What is it?" she asked.

I stepped aside and let her see.

Josie was lying on the floor. Her beekeeper's hat and face net were next to her, revealing her head and a face that was covered with blood.

Sarah screamed. I bent down and found Josie's wrist and tried to feel for a pulse. I couldn't find one. I felt her neck for some indication that her heart still beat. I started to panic. I couldn't feel anything. I held my flashlight closer to her body and then I noticed the pool of blood that was seeping out from behind her head. A trail of blood led from Josie to the back door of the house.

"Go back to the car and get my cell phone. Call 911 and tell Dave to get up here fast and send an ambulance. I think she's dead."

Sarah took the flashlight and hurried out the back screen door. I could hear her gasping as she ran for the car. I sat in the dark next to Josie's body, holding her chilly hand. Then it grew very quiet. Too quiet.

"What am I going to do?" I whispered to myself. I was alone in the dark, with a poor soul who was either dying or dead. I had just about decided to run after Sarah when I thought I heard a noise in the house. Something creaked. I thought I heard footsteps moving away toward the front door. Was someone in there?

Why was Sarah taking so long? A thousand thoughts raced through my mind. I was shaking with fear and shock. Another woman was dead or very close to it. Her secret, the name of Alice's killer and maybe of her own murderer, dead with her. Now we would never learn what she had seen, whom she named as the killer. And maybe that murderer was still in the house. I felt paralyzed with fear. Was I going to be next?

It seemed ages since Sarah had left. Had something happened to her too? Just as I stood up to search for Sarah, I heard someone running toward me along the side of the house. I froze.

Chapter 16

"THEY'RE COMING," Sarah said. "Dave said not to touch anything and to wait in the car with the doors locked. Come on. We can't do her any good anyway. Hurry up, Ellie. It's not safe here. We'll be more secure in the locked car."

I was a little surprised at the coldness of Sarah's words, the disregard of Josie's still cold body, but I knew we shouldn't mess up the crime scene any more than we already had and I, too, was scared of what else could happen. I patted Josie's hand and then left the porch and ran back to the car with Sarah. We got in and locked the doors, turned the headlights on and sat there staring out at the woods. In a few minutes we could hear the sirens bouncing off the hills and echoing down the valley. That was an eerie sound on an eerie night.

We were at Josie's house for what seemed hours, answering Dave's questions and waiting for the State Police to interview us as well.

The paramedics came and left, determining that indeed Josie was dead. They left her where she was; her body would be turned over to the State and the Medical Examiner.

Dave's red face and his clipped voice as he barked out orders let me know just how angry he was feeling. His sweat mingled with the drizzle that had followed the earlier downpour. I had a hard time looking him in the eye. He had confided in me and I had promised to help him and yet I had kept the information about Josie from him. He finally let us go, with the order that I was to be in his office by 9:00 tomorrow for further questioning. Sarah was to appear at her noon break for her interrogation. Sarah and I drove away, feeling sad and miserable.

"Is this our fault?" I asked her. "If we had told Dave, Josie might be alive."

"Stop it Ellie. Don't take that path. She is dead. We had nothing to do with it. It is not our fault."

"But I feel so badly. There must have been some other way than keeping this a secret from Dave. Oh, he must hate us so. I wish I had never opened my door to Josie that night."

The drizzle had turned back into a pouring rain. I turned my wipers on full and listened to the slash, slash as they tried to clear the windshield. Luckily we were not far from my cottage. I pulled in the drive and turned to Sarah.

"Do you want to come in and have some tea and talk? I could use some company."

"No," she answered curtly. "I'm tired. I have to be up by 7:00 which is only in a few hours. I need to go home and get some rest."

I looked at her as I opened the car door. I saw a hard face, etched with deep lines. Sarah's eyes stared straight ahead, not meeting mine. Maybe this has been too much for her. Two women she had known all her life, dead in less than one week. I knew it was too much for me.

As we walked to her car and she opened her door, I wanted to hug her. We had shared a terrible experience together and my instinct told me we needed support from each other. But when I reached out to her, she avoided me by getting into her car and starting the engine.

"Are you all right, Sarah?"

She said, "I'm fine. Just tired. I'll talk to you tomorrow. Goodnight Ellie."

I stood in the rain and watched her red tail lights disappear down the road. I had a bad feeling growing in the pit of my stomach. But it had been a long hard night and I was confused about everything, so I put the instinct away and ran into the house. I was drenched and cold. Despite the time, I got into a hot bath and tried to relax. I willed myself to think about the rain I could hear battering the house and nothing else. I slid down into the tub until only my face was visible. The steam fogged the room and blurred objects and faded reality. I felt so far away from everything, so tired. For a moment I deliberated just sinking all the way down into the hot water and really forgetting the nightmare that I was tangled up in. I closed my eyes and said a prayer for Josie and Alice, for everyone in Hummingbird Falls and for all those I loved. I wished Christopher was here with me, or Sandy and Allison. Loneliness joined my exhaustion and grief.

Chapter 17

IT WAS STILL raining when I woke up. It was late, a little after eight. I remembered that I had to be in Dave's office at 9:00 which left me only an hour to get ready and drive down to town. I decided to skip making coffee and breakfast and just stop in the pastry shop on my way. I threw my trash into the back of my car. I needed to stop at the dump and get rid of any bear tempting smells.

I couldn't believe how hard it was raining. We must have accumulated several inches of rain since last night. It was gray and gloomy out, but no fog obscured the roads, so I could see the washed out areas and was able to avoid them in plenty of time. I noted several sections of road where the creeks had overflowed and were causing the shoulders to disappear. I would report this to Dave and he could let Larry know. At least I could do something positive and helpful. I was worried about what Dave would say to me. I felt like I had really let him and Josie and Hummingbird Falls down.

I stopped in the pastry shop. It was full of chatter and noise that suddenly stopped when I walked in. I felt every eye on me. Were they accusing me of causing Josie's death? That is what it felt like. Cold, distant, stares pierced me. I turned away to the counter. My eyes welled up with tears.

Elizabeth came over to where I was standing. "Oh honey. Don't cry. It must have been just awful for you. We are all so worried about you and Sarah. Are you all right? You weren't hurt were you?"

Without waiting for my answer, she picked out a thick juicy blueberry turnover and handed it to me. "I'll get your coffee. You just go over and sit with Bonnie and Margaret. I'll bring it to you."

Suddenly, Margaret and Bonnie were by my side, putting their arms around me. They led me to their table and handed me a tissue.

"We were so worried about you. How terrible. How can we help?"

I was stunned. This sweet little town was encircling me in its arms. I looked around and everyone was smiling at me or nodding acknowledgement. I couldn't believe it. I had thought they would hate me. Instead, they were tending to me, helping me deal with my own problems. I haven't been one who has been able to ask for help. I have learned to be very independent and deal with my own problems. But here, the people in this town were offering themselves to me, when I needed them, and I didn't even have to ask for the help. I turned around to everyone and whispered a soft "Thank you" through my tears. The crowd responded by offering a quiet applause.

I talked a few minutes with Bonnie and Margaret. They told me that they appreciated the care I had shown for Josie, by going up to her house to visit and check if she was all right. I guessed that was what Dave must have put out on the gossip line. As a result, people were looking at me as if I was some kind of hero, who had unfortunately arrived too late to save their friend. I didn't argue with them because I was just too overwhelmed to explain the true story and I figured if that was what Dave wanted people to believe then he had a reason for it. I excused myself as quickly as I could and Elizabeth put my coffee in a carry out container and wrapped up my uneaten turnover. I waved goodbye to everyone and hurried over to Dave's office.

Dave was waiting for me. He sat tall in his office chair and said, "Sit down, Ellie. We have some talking to do."

No hello or how are you doing? I was even more anxious now. Maybe I had broken some law, or could be accused of being an accomplice after the fact or before the act or what ever they called it.

Dave got up and closed the door. He drew up another office chair and plopped it down close to me. He leaned forward and stared into my face. "Tell me what's been going on, Ellie. I think you know more than you have been letting on. Start from the beginning and don't leave anything out."

And so I did. I started with Josie's visit to my house last Monday night and ended with last night's discovery of her body. I wept in parts of the story. What had seemed colorful or eccentric about Josie just appeared so sad now that she was dead.

When I finished Dave asked, "Is that the whole truth or is there more you aren't telling me?"

"That's it, Dave, I promise. I am so sorry that I didn't come to you first thing. When I talked it over with Sarah, it seemed so right not to talk to you, but I can see now that was completely wrong. I don't know how I got so turned around. But Sarah was so sure we were doing what we had to do to protect Josie and I guess I just trusted her. I should have come to you directly, before anything else. I am so very sorry."

"Well, Ellie, you have to live with that. I don't know what got into you either. Why would you trust Sarah and not me? You should have come to me."

"I know." I was crying now. "Please forgive me. I'm so sorry. Do you think it was my fault that Josie is dead? How could I have been so stupid? This is so terrible. Josie's dead and it's my fault. She would be better off in the state hospital than dead. I should have known better."

I dissolved in tears. Dave did nothing to comfort me. I sat in my own misery. I had gotten myself into this horrible mess and I was the only one who could get me out. I wiped my eyes and nose and looked at Dave.

"Where do we go from here? What can I do to try to make this up to you, to make things right again? I can't bring Josie back. I wish I could, oh, I wish I could. What can I do, Dave?"

"Well, Ellie, I am going to have to think about that. I will tell you that a blow to the head, similar to the blow that killed Alice, killed Josie. The Medical Examiner will determine if they are identical, if the same weapon was used. We are pretty close to identifying the weapon used on Alice."

He continued, "Josie was killed in her house. All the evidence points to that, so we are scouring the house and surroundings for everything that might help lead us to the killer. I'm guessing that the killer was dragging Josie out the back of the house when you arrived there. The killer must have heard you and dropped Josie's body on the screen porch and ran back into the house to hide. I think he went out the front door when you and Sarah went around the back. The front door was unlocked."

"It was locked when we got there. I tried it myself. And I heard someone in the house while I was waiting with Josie for Sarah to come back from calling you from the car. She took so long and I was so afraid someone would come out and get me, too. But the footsteps just moved away from the back door and then I didn't hear anything more."

"Yep, we think he was there when you were. It was a close call. You could have been killed, too. Good thing you didn't see him or you might have been."

That statement hit me hard. I hadn't realized I had been so close to a murderer. I shivered. I was really scared now.

"What should I do, Dave? Do you think he will come after me or Sarah?"

"I don't know, Ellie. I have called in some extra deputies. I will have them keep an eye on your place. There are groups of neighbors who are driving around in shifts, too, to check on folks like you who live alone, or out in the country. If you hear anything suspicious, call. That's about all I can recommend for now."

Dave sat back. He looked so tired and beaten down. He probably hadn't slept in days. I sat in silence with him. Suddenly, I remembered that I hadn't told him about Pauline's confession in the little church.

"Dave, I forgot all about what I came to your office yesterday to tell you. So much has happened so fast that it just flew out of my mind. I think it might be important though."

I quickly recounted what Pauline had said to me yesterday in the Little Church. Dave sat quietly and listened.

"Pauline is on the list of people who I am interviewing today. Thanks for the information, Ellie. I'll follow up on that with her and see if it leads to anything."

"What about our plan for me to try to talk to people who might be suspects, Dave?"

"I believe you have done all the talking you need to, for the time being. I'll think about it and get back to you. Frankly, Ellie, I'm disappointed in the decisions you and Sarah made. You should have known better. Well, we're finished here for now. I'm going to talk to Sarah to get her view of things and I'll get back to you. Be careful, Ellie."

"I am so sorry, Dave. I hope I can rebuild your trust. I feel just awful about this."

Dave gave a weak smile. "Everyone makes mistakes, Ellie. I've made mine and you made yours. The important thing is not to make the same mistake again. I know you were just doing what you thought was right. But from now on, no matter what, you come to me. Can you promise me that?"

"Yes, absolutely. I promise."

"Then, let's move beyond this and concentrate on what matters, catching whoever killed Alice and Josie before someone else ends up dead."

I left Dave's office feeling ashamed and depressed. He was decent enough to call my behavior a mistake, but that didn't make me feel any better.

I headed for Greenberg with my wipers going full blast and my headlights on. The weather was just awful and I longed to go home and curl up in front of my woodstove reading a book and drinking a nice hot cup of tea. I was exhausted from all the anxiety and trauma of last night. I really didn't want to see Alice's lawyer, Mr. Compton, and didn't know if I could deal with any details given the state I was in. But I had made this appointment with Mr. Compton, and to be truthful, I was really curious about the contents of Alice's will. I just hoped there weren't any unpleasant surprises in store for me. I just couldn't handle anything else. I had just about reached the end of my inner resources, my spirit was wilted and my soul mourned for the two women I had known and cared about who were dead, together, cold and alone, on the autopsy tables in the Medical Examiner's office.

Chapter 18

I FOUND MR. Compton's office without any trouble. He and his associates had placed a big green sign with carved and gold gilded letters outside their refurbished colonial home that had been made into an office site. I entered and announced myself to the receptionist and was sent in to see Alice's lawyer.

Mr. Compton went right to the paper work without any chitchat or superficial introductory talk. He clearly was all business. He had me fill out a number of forms and sign papers that he said I really didn't need to read because they were just the usual legal business that was required by the state and IRS when one was named executor of a will. After a half an hour I had finally signed everything that he had ready for me.

Mr. Compton went to his file cabinet and extracted a thick folder. He sat behind his desk and slowly shuffled through the papers in the file. Finally, he extracted a legal size document containing several pages stapled together.

"This is Alice Foster's last will and testament. Over the years Alice made frequent changes to her will. She made the last changes less than a week before she died."

"You mean she came down here last week and made out a new will?"

"Yes, nothing unusual about that. As I said, she changed her will several times over the last few years. I'll read it to you. Once we enter it into probate it is public record, so we will wait until we have notified the beneficiaries before we take that next step. We don't want the newspapers reporting who received what before the actual recipients find out."

"That makes sense," I said. "It was a little different when my husband died, since I was the sole beneficiary and the executrix. There wasn't much to leave and he just had a very simple will."

"Well, this will isn't simple. In fact, as you will find out, it is rather complicated and very well may end up being contested. It might take years before we are finished with the final probate. So, we might as well get started."

He started reading the will, dated just last week. I was a bit dazed after all I had been through and wasn't very attentive through the first part of the will which was the usual, being in sound mind, address, naming executor and other legal, but uninteresting details. Suddenly, I heard something that made me sit up straight and listen hard.

"I leave to my dear friend, Eleanor Hastings, who wants so badly to be a legal resident of our lovely Hummingbird Falls community, thirty acres along Foster's Creek, as is designated on the attached surveyor's map. In addition, I leave Eleanor Hastings, $200,000 to build the house of her choice on those thirty acres. This property and money is free and clear of any limitations or encumbrances and at the time of her death, or any time before, Mrs. Hastings may dispose of the property as she wishes."

Mr. Compton looked up at me. "I guess you weren't expecting that, were you?"

"No," I gasped. "Not at all. I had talked a lot with Alice about trying to find land or a house I could afford, but I never expected this. Oh, dear sweet Alice." I broke down in tears. Mr. Compton excused himself, saying he would bring us both some coffee.

I sat sobbing, stunned, and thought about my wonderful friend Alice, who had listened so well to my dreams and now had brought them to reality. Sometimes, no matter how close we may be to someone, we still don't realize the depth of his or her soul or the sweetness of his or her spirit. She had been planning to gift me with this land, land that I loved and walked with her so many times and she never gave me a clue as to her intention. She was not a woman who wanted thanks or praise. She was generous and altruistic and just wanted to make her friends happy. I felt so blessed.

Mr. Compton entered the room with two coffees and a box of tissue. "Here you go. Let's see if you can get yourself together and we can continue on with this will. Do you think you can manage that? I have appointments lined up all day, so I can't take too much time right now. This is just a cursory reading so you can be heads up. Remember, don't tell anyone but the beneficiaries about the will yet. We will schedule the reading right after the services I hear are planned for the day after tomorrow in Hummingbird Falls. Is that correct?"

"Yes, the services will be followed with a reception afterwards at the Inn. I can book a small conference room at the Inn to use for the reading of the will. I'm able to continue now. I'm just so shocked and so much has happened. I don't promise you I will be all together, but I can try to be as present as possible for the rest of the reading. I do promise I won't say a word to anyone about the will."

"Fine," Mr. Compton said. "I will continue but I will skip over certain portions that are relevant only to the specific beneficiary. Alice has included quite a few personal remarks to individuals, although I cautioned her not to do so. Of course, the entire will has to be read to the beneficiaries, but right now, for us, we only need to touch on the highlights. The beneficiaries I mention should be notified immediately and told to be at the meeting. You can take care of that, right? Of course, I will be there. I will read the will, but you must be there, too."

Skimming down through the typed lines, with an expression of grimness, Mr. Compton grabbed my attention. He started reading again. "To my friend, Pauline Hayes, jot that name down. Do you know her?"

"Yes. I will call her."

"Next is James Foster, Alice's half-brother. Do you know him?"

"No. But I have talked to him once about Alice's service. He is staying at Alice's so I will call him there. Go on."

"Margaret Joyner, owner of the Hummingbird Falls Gallery."

"Yes. I can talk to her."

"David and Mary Shaffer."

"OK. I've got them on the list."

"Colby Conners."

"What did you say?" I asked.

"Colby Co   . That young man you were sitting with in the pastry shop, if I am not mistaken."

"Yes, but why Colby?"

"I'm not able to reveal client personal information, only the wishes she expressed in the will. Can you contact Colby Conners?"

"Yes," I said, shaking my head in disbelief.

"Let me see, the Town Manager of Hummingbird Falls, the Little Church, the Hummingbird Falls Library, Historical Society, and Elementary School, the Green Mountain Conservation Alliance, Audubon, the Heart and Cancer Foundations, the Family Violence Center, several other charitable foundations. I will notify those people with official letters. They don't need to have a representative at the reading."

"OK," I said. All the groups that were mentioned stunned me. I never knew Alice was so well off.

"Oh, one more. Mr. Arnold Wilson. Do you know him?"

"No."

"He is the brother of a Mr. Wilson who was murdered about thirteen years ago. His sister-in-law and niece were killed too. I believe he is listed in the phone book. He moved into his brother's house after everything settled down."

"He's a beneficiary?"

"Yes. Notify him. If you have any trouble reaching any of these people, let me know. The will stipulates that they all must be gathered at the same time or the will can't be read. I'd like to get this accomplished as quickly as we can before everyone gets scattered."

"I will call him, too," I said. "Anyone else?"

"Let me look it over again to see if I missed anyone. Oh yes, Michael Greeley of Hummingbird Falls, Josie Webster, and Sarah Moody. That's it. Will you call them?"

"I can call Mike and Sarah," I said. Then the tears came again. "But Josie was found dead last night, murdered in her own home."

"My God. What is going on up on that mountain? First Alice is killed and then another woman. Well, if Josie Webster is deceased, her gift goes into the general account. I'll explain that later. That's all. I hope we can get them all accounted for and t   er. I'm leaving that part up to you. You have to earn your money somehow." He laughed.

"What do you mean earn my money?"

"As executor you are entitled to 6% of the total assets of Alice Foster. You are going to be pretty well off."

"I don't believe it," I stammered.

Mr. Compton stood up. "Call my secretary when you have talked to everyone on the list. If there are no problems, I will see you after the service at the Inn. Are you all set? Any questions?"

"Not right now, I guess. I am just so overwhelmed by it all. I will call them and then call your office. Then I will see you at the Inn. I'll reserve the room. Thank you, Mr. Compton. I am really going to need your help."

"That's fine. My time is paid out of Ms. Foster's resources. So call on me all you want."

I left the office in a daze. I almost forgot to turn off the road to the dump. Only the smell of my bags of trash reminded me of my next stop. Hummingbird Falls shares the dump with Greenberg. If you live in Greenberg you receive a green sticker for your windshield and if you are from Hummingbird Falls your sticker is red with a hummingbird embossed on it. When you enter the dump, there is one compacter marked Greenberg which is painted green and right next to it, another compactor painted red and marked Hummingbird Falls. The dump attendant watches carefully that only cars with matching stickers throw their garbage in the appropriate trash compactor. All over the dump are various signs telling patrons what to do. No glass or cardboard in the trash compactor and no building materials or brush. There are separate piles for furniture, mattresses, building supplies, metal, and brush. In addition, only glass is to be thrown in the metal dumpster, only plastic in the barrel and only cans in the bucket of the big dozer. A sign informs patrons that inside are the "treasures." Old TV's, vacuums, clothes, books, and a bit of everything else that is still fixable or usable is displayed for the taking. I always check the treasures when I go to the dump. Sometimes I find wonderful items that others have rejected, but are just what I want or need.

No one else was there when I arrived. The rain must have discouraged the dump pickers. I backed into the Hummingbird Falls' allotted space and turned off my car. I slumped over the steering wheel and just dissolved in tears. I cried for a long time. The rain from the sky and the tears from my eyes seemed unending.

Finally, I pulled myself together and opened the car door, gathered the garbage bags and threw them one by one down into the nearly empty pit. With each bag I used a little more force until I was slamming the bags against the steel walls of the pit. The violent sounds matched the anger I felt rising in me. I wanted to smash and crush and destroy. I wanted to feel strong, stronger than the evil killer who was slowly destroying the beauty of Hummingbird Falls.

When every trace of trash was gone from my car, I climbed back in. I realized I was feeling a little bit better now. The adrenaline

100

flow from the anger had energized me a bit. I decided to drive over to the treasures' building when something moving next to the metal pile caught my eye.

A medium size black mutt was limping toward me. It was drenched, hair matted and very thin. It looked sick and hurt. I hesitated a moment, looking around for the dump attendant. The dog came closer. Several cases of rabies had been reported in this area, mostly in raccoons and foxes, and I knew everyone had to be careful of stray dogs, just in case they had had a run in with an infected animal. I started my car and drove to the treasure shed. I hurried in before the dog could reach me.

Chapter 19

DENNY, THE DUMP man, was sitting next to the wood stove reading, of all things, a Smithsonian Magazine. I wondered if it were one of mine that I had put into the recycling bin for books and magazines last week.

"Hi, Denny," I said. "I was wondering. There's a sorry looking mutt out there in the rain. Have you seen him?"

"Yeah. He showed up here a couple of days ago. I've been trying to catch him. I've put food out for him and he comes late at night and eats it, but he won't let me near him. Guess I have to call the Humane Society to pick him up. Probably a lost dog, chasing a rabbit and strayed too far from home. Or maybe, some visitor opened the car door and he escaped and took off. It happens every year. We end up with half grown dogs in fall that were sweet puppies in spring. A lot of the tourists adopt a puppy at the beginning of the season and then just leave it to fend for itself when they go back to the city. It's sickening, if you ask me."

"That's terrible," I said. I looked out the window. The dog was just standing in the rain, shaking, holding his left back leg up. "He's hurt. Do you think he's sick or infected?"

"Can't be sure, of course. But he doesn't look like he has rabies. Just hungry, hurt and lost. He hasn't bothered anyone. He seems to approach the women who come to the dump more than the men. He's shy, like he has been abused or mistreated. He doesn't have a collar, but he does have what looks to be a rabies tag on a small chain around his neck. So, someone must have vaccinated him. Whether it's up to date or not, I don't know."

"I think I'm going to try to lure him over to my car. Do you have any dog food or biscuits?"

"Here, try this." Dennis produced an open tin can of dog food. He gave me an old bent spoon and a tin plate from the treasure table. "Good luck. But be careful. He could turn on you. I'll watch from in here where I can stay dry if you don't mind."

"Thanks Dennis. If I do catch him, I'll take him to the vet right away."

I stepped out the door into the rain, which was falling even heavier now. The wind chilled the air. It was not a good time to be hurt and outside. I took a couple of steps toward the dog and bent down and spooned the dog food onto the plate and put it on the ground and pushed it toward the dog.

"Come on, boy. Come and get it. It's good. I won't hurt you. Come on."

The dog just stared at me. We were both soaked and dripping and cold. I inched a little closer, crooning to the dog. "Come on Buddy. Take a taste. It's good."

The dog sniffed and looked longingly at the plate. I sat still and called him softly.

"It's all yours. Come get it. Come, let me pet you. Poor dog. You're all wet."

The dog took a step closer and watched me. When I didn't move, he took another step and then another until he could reach the

102

plate of food. Before eating, he studied me. I stayed as still as I could with the cold rain dripping into my eyes, off my chin and down my neck. The poor animal was trembling with cold and fear.

He started to gulp the food down. I reached forward and grabbed the thin chain around his neck, so he couldn't run off. He looked at me and tried to back away, but didn't show any teeth. He was shaking and his brown eyes seemed sad and desperate. I patted his dirty wet coat and continued my soft murmur of nonsense to him. He seemed to calm a bit. He looked back at the plate of food. I edged the plate closer to him.

"Go ahead, boy. Eat it up. There will be more for you at home. You must be hungry, Buddy."

He put his head down and scoffed up the food. Then he looked at me and whined. I stood up and led him to my car. When I opened the door, to my surprise, he hopped right in the front seat and sat down. I turned and waved to Dennis who was watching us from the window and got in the car. Just at that moment, the dog stood up and shook. Dirty droplets of water and mud flew all over me and the inside of the car. What a mucky mess. I drove down the steep hill from the dump, wondering what I had got myself into now.

What was I thinking of, picking up this dirty sick stray dog? With all that was going on, I now had taken on the responsibility of a dog, now shivering in my front seat. Sometimes I just don't know how I get into these situations. I sighed, turned on the heater full blast and drove straight to the local veterinary clinic. Luckily Helen, the young vet, was between patients and could see Buddy and me right away. She laughed at our grubby appearance.

"I don't know who looks worse, you or the dog. You look like you belong together, that's for sure."

We went into an exam room. Helen checked Buddy out and found that he was running a temperature.

"Probably from that infected wound on his foot. He must have cut a pad a while ago and picked up an infection. He's vaccinated for rabies, so that's not a problem. I really don't see much else that's wrong except that he's underweight. Hasn't eaten well for a while, I'd guess. Probably a stray or abandoned. Do you want me to call the Humane Society? They'll hold him for a while. But this time of year, not too many dogs are adopted, I'm afraid, especially half grown ones. People just seem to want the puppies. They will keep him for a while and if no one wants him or claims him, they have to put him down."

"Oh, no. I don't want him killed. Can I take him? I've been thinking about getting a dog."

"I don't see why not, as long as you inform the refuge and Humane Society that you have found the dog, just in case someone is looking for him. He's better off with you than in a kennel. I'll fill him full of antibiotics and give you some pills to give him three times a day for the next week. That should clear the infection and get him back on all four feet."

Ellie asked, "Do you think he has a good disposition? I don't want a mean dog."

"He looks like he'll be a nice dog. He didn't give me any trouble during the exam. He's used to being handled. I guess he ran from Dennis because he was being chased, poor dog. He probably didn't know what to do, all on his own, other than follow his nose to the smell of rotting food."

"Okay, then. I'll take him."

"{Congratulations on your new dog. Did I hear you call him Buddy? That's a great name. I'll enter that on his file chart and give you the pills and you bring him back to see me next week and we will give him another check over and any shots he needs and heart worm medication. Any problems, call."

"Thanks Doctor. I guess his name is Buddy. He's awfully sweet, isn't he? And after a bath, I bet he'll be beautiful."

I set out for the drive home, not even minding the pounding rain. I had Buddy to keep me company and he was content to curl up in the front seat and sigh and then go to sleep, comforted by the warm air of the heater. I thought of that old saying, you had better be careful of what you ask for, because you might just get it. I had been wishing for a dog to help protect me and here Buddy was. Sometimes the world is just like that.

Chapter 20

I HAD BUDDY in the tub before he knew what was happening. Three times I had to empty the tub and start with fresh water. He was filthy, but compliant. I noticed a few ticks, fleas and various other debris floating in the tub after the first wash. But the fourth tub of water remained pretty clean and I knew we had finished with the bathing project. I just needed to towel Buddy off, comb him out and put on the tick and flea repellant. Then Buddy could eat and rest and we could get to know each other.

I sat down in a chair, exhausted, and watched Buddy eat a full bowl of the dry food I had bought at the vets. He burped, looked around and then climbed up into my lap to settle down. I laughed and pushed him back down to the floor. But the look on his face drove me to move to the couch and pat the cushion next to me. Up he came, lay down and put his head in my lap. I patted him and soon he was fast asleep, making little twitches and jerks as he dreamed away.

I had other things to do, so I gently put his head on the cushion and eased myself off the couch and walked toward the phone. I had only gone a few steps when I heard the pat pat of Buddy's toenails on the hardwood floor. I turned and there he was, looking up at me. I had a Buddy, for sure. I was going to have to adjust to this new element of my life. I wasn't used to being followed around, or stared at in my own home. I had lived alone so long, I wasn't sure how Buddy's presence was going to affect me.

I checked my messages. I had several concerning the service for Alice, one from Dave, and several hang-ups. Without caller ID I had no idea who the hang-ups were. I worried that my son Sandy might have called me again. But if so, why didn't he leave a message? I was unsure whether I should call him. So, I put off that decision and instead I quickly took care of the inquiries about Alice's service, booked a conference room at the Inn for the reading of the will, and then called Dave.

"What's up, Dave?" I asked after being connected.

"Ellie, I have received some information from the Medical Examiner that is highly confidential. I want to know if you still are interested in consulting with me on this case and if you can play by the rules of disclosure and confidentiality."

"Dave, I promise you. I have learned my lesson. I want to help. Thanks for giving me a second chance."

"OK, but don't make me regret this, please. The ME found that the cause of death was identical for both Alice and Josie. The weapon is the same or very similar and left almost identical indenting on both skulls. She thinks the weapon is an iron rod, about one half inch round with a curved ending. Perhaps similar to those iron plant hangers that people use on their porches for flower pots or stake in their yards to hold bird feeders and such."

"That makes it hard. So many people have hanging flowerpot rods. How can we find out who has the one which is the weapon?"

"Well, this rod is unique in that it appears to be hand crafted, round not flat, curled on the end, and only one half inch round. That should eliminate a lot of the other rods, most of which are machine made. Of course, the killer could have thrown it away or buried it, but the fact that it was used twice in a span of days means the killer kept it after the first murder. Maybe still has it. We can hope so."

"So, if I turn conversations around to the subject of iron smithing, or iron crafts, or ways people hang things, I might get some leads?"

"Well, that's about all we have at this point. I'm still conducting interviews with everyone who saw Alice or talked to her before her death. Colby is tracking down any suspicious people or cars that have been reported and checking hotel and inn registrations for any known felons. I am talking to James Foster tomorrow. He agreed to come in when I talked to him after the meeting last night."

"That should be helpful," I said.

"I hope so, Ellie. I really hope so. So, if you could start asking around subtly about that rod, I would appreciate it. Remember, the murder weapon is not being released to the press or public yet, so be discreet. Call me if you get anything. I'll be in touch."

I put down the phone and sat down. I was relieved that Dave still trusted in me, but I felt pressure to discover something about the murder weapon. What was the best way to go about chatting with people about forged iron? That certainly had never entered into my conversations before. I had better research the subject before I made a fool of myself and gave people reason to be suspicious of me.

I spent the next hour on the internet finding out more than I ever wanted to about black smithing, the qualities of iron, the types of hangers forged, sources, retailers, prices, local iron workers and so on. Finally, I closed down my computer and rubbed my eyes. It was time for bed.

I almost forgot about Buddy. I turned the motion light on, and let him out in the yard to do his business. I stood on the porch and watched him cavort and smell and mark his territory. The rain didn't seem to bother him now, with a good meal in his stomach, and he rambled about as well as he could on three legs. He found a very interesting scent back by the hemlocks that lined a little stream on the edge of the cleared yard. His hair bristled and I could hear him growl deep in his throat.

I called him and clapped my hands. Only reluctantly did he turn and limp back to the porch. I would have to get him a leash. I was afraid he would run off after some animal and get lost. I brought him inside and fed him his medicine and turned out the lights and locked the doors. Buddy and I walked into the bedroom and Buddy jumped up on the bed and made himself comfortable. I sighed. Change wasn't one of my favorite things. I figured I would deal with it after my shower and tooth brushing. But when I came back into the bedroom, Buddy was asleep and he had left room for me, so I just slipped into the bed. Somehow, I felt safer with him there and as long as he didn't try to take over, I thought we would do just fine.

Chapter 21

IT WAS POURING again. Ever since Buddy and I got up the rain had been dashing against our windows, then dripping and then slashing at them once again. I had started a fire in the wood stove to try to keep the clammy dampness from seeping into everything and Buddy found the fire very inviting. I attended to my chores when I wasn't looking out the windows wondering what more rain meant to the roads, the falls and rivers, and the village itself.

I found my pile of mail where I had set it yesterday. I had completely forgotten about it. I reached for the letter from my daughter and opened it.

Dear Mom,

I don't exactly know how to tell you this, so I'll just write it out fast. I couldn't call you to tell you because I knew I would just break down and cry.

I've lost my job. Really, I was kind of fired. Then I quit. Two weeks ago. I didn't have the nerve to tell you until now. In fact, I wasn't going to tell you at all until I got another job. But I haven't found one yet. I have a couple of interviews lined up, but they don't seem too promising either.

The truth is, I need some money. My rent's due next week and my bank account is down to nothing. I hate to ask you. I know you've been on a fixed income and having a hard time making ends meet yourself, so it is very hard to ask you for money. I wouldn't ask if I had any other source, but I'm flat out. Could you help me? It would be a loan, of course. I won't accept any money unless we agree that it's a loan. I think $2000 would be enough for now. That'll pay my rent and car payment and give me a little for food. I can let the utilities go for a while. I should find a job soon, I hope.

I love you, Mom and I'm sorry I have to ask you for this favor. I hope I haven't created a bad ripple in what is always a heavenly, peaceful vacation for you in your beautiful mountains. If you can't afford to loan me the money now, don't worry. I'll find a way. Xxoo Love, Allison

"Oh no," I whispered. "Now the other one's in trouble."

How could this be? Allison had always had a top notch job in her field of research marketing. She earned what seemed a huge salary to me. Much more than I had ever earned as a school teacher. Why had she been fired? I went directly to the phone and called her. The answering machine picked up. I left a message for her to call me as soon as she could and that of course I would help her. I told her I loved her and tried to assure her that everything would be all right. Then I tried her cell phone. I was informed that the cell phone account had been discontinued. This was another shock. Allison was totally attached and dependent on her cell phone. I couldn't believe she would give it up. So much of her work contacting people was when she was on the go. What in the world was going on with her? Now I would have to wait to hear from her. I tried her home phone again, just on a chance that she would pick it up. Only the answer machine responded. I hung up dismayed. Both my children were in a mess.

I patted Buddy and he licked my face. "I guess you're doing okay at least." I swear he smiled at me while he banged his tail against the couch cushion. I decided that instead of just waiting and worrying about the kids that I would try to follow up on the forged iron rod clue. I planned to visit several of the garden and gift shops in the area to see what they had for sale. The weather was so bad that I decided I would call Larry and ask about the road conditions before I set out.

The phone rang several times, and then was answered by a young voice I didn't recognize.

"Is Larry there?"

"No. He and the whole crew are out working on the Falls Road. Can I help you?"

"Who are you?" I asked.

"Sorry. This is Bobby Brady. I am on phone dispatch while the rest of them are out trying to clean up the worst roads."

"That's what I am calling about. How are the roads from Durkin Farm Road down into town?"

"The last I heard was that the Falls Road is closed, but you could take the Notch Road. It has a few wash outs, but the road is passable if you're careful, or was when Larry last called in. But the shoulders are dangerous, just about gone in some places, washed down hill. So be on the lookout and stay toward the center of the road. We are watching the lower bridge. The river is rising pretty fast. But the bridge is still open."

"Thanks, Bobby. By the way, this is Ellie Hastings. How are you doing now?"

"I don't mind saying that I'm better than before. I have been having awful nightmares of that face, but not as often as before. I'm still pretty shaken up. Thanks for asking."

"You're welcome, Bobby. I know your job is not always easy, but to find a body in the falls must have been terrible for you."

"I guess you understand how it is, Ms. Hastings. Wasn't it you who found old crazy Josie dead up at her house?"

I took offense at his description of Josie and said rather defensively, "I wouldn't want to categorize her by calling her old and crazy." Then remembering that Bobby was only sixteen, I added, "Although she was an older woman with some mental health problems. But yes, I found her. And like you, I'm not taking it too well. It's quite a shock to discover someone dead. How did you hear that I found her?"

"Oh, some of the guys were talking about it. They said that whoever killed Miss Foster probably killed old Josie. They are saying we have a serial killer because there wasn't any reason to kill them and no robbery or anything. They say none of the women around here are safe until this guy is caught. They think it might be that James Foster, Miss Foster's brother. Nothing happened until he came, not since the Wilson murders. Of course, I don't remember that. I was only three when all those murders took place."

"What did they say about the Wilson murders, Bobby?"

"Not much, just that James Foster disappeared right around that time and that Callie Wilson was his girl friend."

"Really? I wasn't here then either. I hadn't heard that Callie Wilson was his girlfriend. Did they think he killed her back then?"

"You'd have to ask Larry. I don't know. I didn't listen to their conversation all that closely. Something about that James left without telling anyone that he was going soon after the Wilson's were all killed. I really don't know much about it."

"Thanks, Bobby. You are doing a good job on the phones. I will come to town by the Notch Road and I'll watch out for the shoulders. Bye."

Another little piece of information had found its way to me. So James Foster had been seeing Callie Wilson who was murdered along with her father and mother thirteen years ago. He left town after the murders. Her skull was found far away from her father and mother's massacred bodies. Could James have killed them? Maybe he wanted Callie to go out with him and her parents refused, so he killed them and dragged her off and then killed her. Then James disappeared and showed up thirteen years later and killed another two women, one his half sister. If he had killed before, then wasn't he more likely to kill again? This theory was rather far fetched, but had potential.

Dave was interviewing him this morning. I wondered what he found out. After I drove down to the pastry shop I would stop by the Police Station and see if Dave was available.

Buddy and I ran to the car under my umbrella. Buddy shook himself thoroughly once he was inside the car, but this time I had my rain slicker on and didn't care. Plus, Buddy was clean now, so his shake offs were just like an extra sprinkle of rain. We took the Notch Road into town and like Bobby had told me, the road was in pretty bad shape. If the Falls Road was worse, it was impassable and dangerous. Once the river gets so high that it runs over onto the road, then a whole other cascade of water forms. The asphalt serves as a smooth riverbed and the water can rush down, flooding houses on both sides of the road. And having no obstacles other than curves, the water has an easy downhill flow right into the heart of town. I had heard this only happened one other time in Hummingbird Falls, a long while ago. But it was possible.

Once again the pastry shop was filled. Everyone was talking about the rain and the trouble spots in town. For now, the murders of Alice and Josie were rendered second to the newest crisis. Mike Greeley was sitting in a booth with a few other farmers and talking loudly. I overheard him as I was waiting for my turnover and coffee.

"I'm gonna get cut off up there on the mountain. Already my road is gone. A ditch four feet wide is across where the culvert used to be. Luckily I parked my truck at the bottom of the drive last night and walked on up to the house. This morning I drove down to the ditch in my old Subaru. So I have a vehicle on either side and just have to climb down into the ditch and ford the stream and get in the other vehicle. My granddad used that trick years ago when the water was high. Right now the Alder Creek is running through my road and making a mess of my lower field. If this keeps up, the Wentworth House just below me will be in trouble. I came down to town on the Scranton Road that runs by Skitter Brook and that little brook is roaring and just about up on the road, too. We could be in a mess of trouble if this damn rain doesn't stop. Let alone, no one can hay. First cutting is no good, too wet. If it doesn't stop soon we won't have a second cutting either."

Farmers weren't the only ones who would be affected by the rain. Woodsmen can't cut or haul timber in heavy rain. Their machinery gets mired down. Livestock is more difficult to tend to. Gift shops and galleries are dependent on the tourists that good weather brings. So are the restaurants, inns, golf courses, bars, boat rentals, antique shops, and all the people who earn their livings working in those seasonally driven occupations. Not only can the rain destroy the landscapes, but the economy as well. Two murdered women in one week with an unknown killer running about didn't help matters either. Hummingbird Falls was on the edge of a disaster.

I sat down with Debbie from the town offices. She was as plain as her cohort Bonnie was pretty. She was married to a logger and had three children. Her mother babysat for her kids while she worked. She wore a constant smile on her thin face and I had never heard her disagree about anything.

"Debbie, what's the news you are hearing at the Town Offices today? Is everyone worried about the rain?"

"Sure are. The town manager called the State DOT to see what we need to do to file for disaster help or extra funds to help repair the roads. Then we have a call into FEMA in Washington, DC to find out funds they have if we do have a flood disaster. Bonnie is talking to the Red Cross, but it seems this whole area is affected, not just Hummingbird Falls, so I don't know how much help we will get. I guess we are at the tip of the trouble and it gets worse as it goes downstream."

"Gosh, this sounds really serious."

"Not yet, it isn't. But we have to be prepared just in case it gets worse. If it stopped raining tomorrow and didn't rain again for a week, we would be OK. Another few days like today, though and we have to call out all the forces we can get."

"Alice's funeral service is tomorrow. Do you think we should cancel it?"

"Not yet. Larry will let us know when things need to shut down or evacuations begin. He calls those shots and he hasn't said anything yet."

"Larry seems very capable. I heard he does all his own repair work on the plows and machinery. Does he do other iron work, like for a hobby, in his off time?"

"Yes, as a matter of fact, he's quite a talented man. He does all kind of crafting of rod iron ornaments. I have some myself. He sells them at a good price to people he knows. I think he likes to make them more than sell them. I have a bird food hanger he made. He put a special curl on the hanger part. It's real pretty. He's making some hinges for my kitchen cabinets. I want them to look kind of rustic. He's good at that."

"Do you know anyone else who does iron work or sells handcrafted iron works?"

"Several curio and gift shops in town carry that type of thing. Heppie's flower shop has some in the garden section that are nice. I think Larry may sell out of those shops, but others might too. I just don't know who they might be. Why?"

"I'm looking for a hand crafted hanger for my porch that could hold a large potted plant. I want a hand forged one with a rod about a half an inch in diameter with a little curl on the end. Have you seen any like those?"

"Yes, sounds like Larry's work. Check with him. To change the subject, did you know that Dave was interrogating James Foster this morning?"

I played dumb. Debbie was so eager to be the one who passed on this juicy piece of information. "No," I said. "What happened?"

"I saw him come in and I saw him go out about an hour later, all in a huff. But upstairs we can't hear what goes on down in the Police station, unless there are shots, which there weren't, or there is loud yelling, which there was." She had a gleam in her eye as she looked at me. So I urged her on by opening my mouth and eyes wide as I could and saying,

"No! Tell me. You have the most exciting job!"

Debbie bent forward to whisper to me. "Of course, this is highly private, so don't pass it on. But I did hear a lot of yelling from down there just before James ran out. I thought there might have been a fight. I didn't hear Dave's voice. He usually stays pretty calm. But James was yelling things like, 'you won't get me for this.' And 'you've got nothing, no evidence at all.' And then lots of language that I can't repeat."

"What did you think, Debbie? What made James so mad?"

"Well, I did have to go down and use the ladies room at one point, and I heard Dave say he would nail him for murder if he did it. James yelled that he didn't do anything now or then. I don't know exactly what he meant by that, but someone else had to use the bathroom and so I went back upstairs. I think Dave is accusing James Foster of killing his sister and I think he's right. Don't you?"

"I don't know, Debbie. Do you think he would have killed Josie, too?"

"Only reason he would have murdered Josie is if she saw something that made James look bad. But we won't know now, will we? Poor Josie. Are you planning her service, too?"

"No. The ladies at the Little Church are doing that. It's going to be the day after Alice's service, on Monday, so we can use the same flowers, and some of the food left over from the reception. I guess Josie's service and reception will be simple, small, and just held in the church itself. She didn't have any family. The reception will be in the Sunday School room."

"Poor Josie," said Debbie. "Well, I have to go back to work now. Bonnie will be in for her break soon. I'll tell her you're here."

"Don't bother. I have to do some errands. Maybe I'll stop over and say hello to you both later."

Debbie said, "That would be great. On days like today, all the breaks we can get are welcomed. You can't imagine the calls we have been getting, both about the murders and about the weather. Our office is chaotic; everyone rushing about, let alone the falls and the rivers."

I drove over to the police station. Dave was free so I went in his office and shut the door. "I am here on official business. As Alice Foster's executrix, I have to inform you that you and your wife are beneficiaries. Her will is being read after the service, during the reception, and all the beneficiaries must be present. Can you both be there?"

I saw the look of surprise on his face. Clearly he was as unprepared for this information as I had been. "Sure we will be there. But beneficiaries? That doesn't make sense. Why would Alice leave something to Mary and me? I have known her all my life and Mary and I were her friends, good friends, I believe. But to leave us something? That's pretty surprising."

"I think Alice may have been full of more surprises than we expected," I said. Before Dave could quiz me on what I meant I asked him, "How did it go with James this morning?"

"Not so good," Dave sighed. "He's as defensive as they get and he has a huge chip on his shoulder about the past, his family and how this town has treated him. I barely got any information from him before he blew up. I have no right to hold him. I don't have any evidence of his guilt, only a feeling. Maybe after the will is read, we will have a motive, at least. I'm pretty sure James, as only kin, will collect most everything,"

"I don't know about that. Isn't the way he acted suspicious? Can't you use that as evidence he has something to hide? Did you find out why he came back?"

"Yes, or at least I think so. He said Alice contacted him and asked him to come back. She wouldn't tell him why, only that it had something to do with the family estate and holdings. He said nothing less would have made him come back to this town. But he claims she put off talking to him about the estate and tried to talk about old matters that he didn't want to relive. They had terrible fights and he would go off into the hills hiking on his own until he cooled down. He said he had loved his sister but over the years, with no response to his letters, he just let his feelings for her and this town go. He swore he never knew his father was sick or when he died. Said the same about his mother. He was never notified, according to him. I don't know whether to believe that or not. Perhaps Sarah would know if mail for Alice arrived from James."

"Who else are you talking to?" I asked.

"I have a several folks lined up this afternoon. I couldn't get anyone to come in yesterday like I planned. So I have to interview Margaret, Mike, Pauline and Colby in that order. I have some others lined up before the service tomorrow. So far, Ellie, I have next to nothing. Did you find out about the rod iron pole?"

"Not much yet. Larry makes them and sells them. They are carried in the local shops and are used mostly for hanging things on outside, birdfeeders, flowers and such. There are other crafters who make the same sort of holder or hanger. I have to buy one of Larry's and compare it with some others and bring them in so you can send them to the ME."

"Good start, Ellie. Larry, hmmm. I knew he did that sort of thing, but his name didn't click before. Why don't you go see him when he's off duty and check it out a little more? Will you?"

"Sure, will do. I know he's really busy up at the Falls Road today, trying to keep the river in its banks and the road where it belongs, but I'll find a way. Good luck with the interviews this afternoon."

"Thanks. If we just keep getting a little bit here, a little bit there, it will soon add up into something that makes sense. At least that is what I hope."

Buddy had been so good waiting for me while I was in the pastry shop and in Dave's office that I decided to reward him with a big bone from the deli-butcher store, which Reggie owned.

No sooner had I walked in then I saw James Foster standing at the deli counter. I walked over to him and introduced myself.

"I hope to see you at the service tomorrow," I said.

"I haven't made up my mind," he mumbled, studying the macaroni salad.

"Well, I need to inform you that the reading of Alice's will is during the reception at the Inn. And since you are one of the beneficiaries, you will need to be present. All the beneficiaries must be there or the will cannot be read."

"What do you mean, all the beneficiaries?" he stormed. "I am the only beneficiary. And who are you to tell me anything about a will? Are you her lawyer?"

"Calm down, James, please. We don't want everyone to know about this, do we? I am the executrix of your sister's will. I have met with her lawyer, Mr. Compton, who will read the will tomorrow to all the beneficiaries."

"You keep saying beneficiaries. I am the only beneficiary and I have Alice's last will and testament to prove it." James was so red I thought his blood pressure must be over the dangerous line. He was sweating and every part of his body was in motion.

"Don't you all try to pull a fast one on me. I know none of you like me and blame me for everything. But you were wrong then and you are wrong now. It is all mine. I deserve it. It was my family that owned it all. So, rightfully, it is mine."

I quietly said, "James, I suggest you contact Mr. Compton in Greenberg. He will explain the circumstances to you. I hope you will show up for the reading. Mr. Compton said there were a great many personal messages from Alice to the beneficiaries and it might be helpful if you heard what she had to say to you. And, I do hope you will come to the service as well. We all loved Alice and the service will be beautiful, I'm sure."

James stared at me, then with a cry of fury, walked through the deli door. Reggie shook his head at me and I shrugged my shoulders at him.

"I'll take a big juicy bone for my dog, Buddy," I said. "He's had a hard morning and he deserves a good treat."

"Coming up," said Reggie. "And how about a nice steak for you? I think maybe you had a hard morning, too."

So, Buddy and I headed up the hill in the downpour, trying to avoid the washed out spots and the rivers of rain that flowed downhill. I could tell Buddy smelled a special reward sitting in the brown bag and I swear he smiled at me again. I could use a bite of steak myself, I thought and looked forward to the rest of the day curled up in our little cottage, warm, full, comfortable and out of the relentless rain.

Chapter 22

BUDDY WAS ENJOYING his bone in front of the wood stove, crunching and munching to his heart's content. I had finished my late lunch of steak and corn on the cob, done up the dishes and was watching Buddy's delight as I figured out my next move in helping to solve the mysteries of Hummingbird Falls. First, who killed Alice and why? Josie had certainly been eliminated as a suspect. Second, who killed Josie and why? Third, what was going on with Margaret, Colby, Pauline, and James

Foster? They were the most likely known suspects thus far, based on their behaviors, but what motive did each of them have? That was beyond me. I had only known the people in this town for ten years. I was missing the history that each carried and it may be that the history contained the motive that was so illusive to me.

I knew that Colby and Pauline had been close in high school, but had broken up when Colby wanted to see other women. Pauline still pined for him, had helped him to search for his birth mother, and carried guilt for someone's death, which she felt she was responsible for. Her story was a confusing mess with too much missing information for me to make sense of it. Maybe it would be a good idea to talk to Pauline again and try to drag more of the story from her. After all, she had started to tell me something in the church before we were interrupted. And I had to talk to her about the meeting for reading the will, as she was a beneficiary. I had better do that right away.

I also needed to get back in contact with Sarah. I didn't understand why she had turned so cold on the night we found Josie dead and we hadn't spoken since. She was a beneficiary, so I had to call her anyway. That would help to start off our conversation. I had to contact Mr. Wilson as well. I started there.

Mrs. Wilson answered the phone. She explained that her husband was at work. I told her about the reading of the will and that her husband was a beneficiary. She didn't even react. She told me that she would relay the message and hung up. That was peculiar, I thought. Everyone else I had contacted was shocked, surprised, or at least showed a strong reaction. Mrs. Wilson had no reaction and asked no questions. Maybe she was just an odd duck.

I dialed the library. Pauline answered. "Pauline, I have to talk with you. I have some important information to share with you. Are you busy down at the library today? I could come down there to meet with you if that is easier."

Pauline hesitated. "Ellie, about the other day, in the church. I was just so upset; I didn't know what I was babbling about. Please just forget it, could you? It isn't my business to talk to anyone about Colby's problems."

"Pauline, rest assured." I avoided answering her directly. I didn't want her to know I had mentioned her conversation to Dave. I needed more information from her.

"I didn't say anything to Chuck about it and I won't. Feel free to talk to me anytime you want. We all need someone to share our troubles with. Talking helps with the pain. But I want to talk to you about something different today, if that's all right. Can I come down?"

"The library's deserted today. The rain's keeping everyone at home, I think. Even the kid's korner reading group was cancelled this morning. I can see the bottom of the falls out the front window and the water's moving higher and higher. I'm planning to move some of the books to the higher shelves, so I will be busy, but I could use some help with that if you don't mind talking and shelving books at the same time."

"I'd be glad to help. Do you mind if I bring my dog Buddy along? I just got him and I don't want to leave him alone too long. He's well behaved."

"Sure, bring him along. I'd like to meet him. How sweet you got a dog, Ellie. And smart. With two women murdered, getting a dog makes sense. I'd get one too, only my father won't have it. He hates animals."

"I'll tell you the story of Buddy when I get there. And, oh yes, I can tell you my bear story too. I have one now. I'll be there in about an hour. The roads are getting pretty bad, so I have to take it slow."

"Drive carefully, Ellie. It can be dangerous with all this rain."

Next I called Sarah at the Post Office. The phone rang and rang and finally an answering machine informed me that my call would be answered as soon as possible and to leave a message. I waited for the beep and then told Sarah it was urgent that I talk to her today and could we meet after she finished work? I asked her to call me as soon as possible and told her I was headed down to town and would try to stop in the Post Office to talk with her.

I tried my son Sandy's number, but only got the answering machine so I hung up. On second thought, it was probably better to wait for him to call me. I didn't want to interfere unless I was asked, but I was worried about how he and Marilyn were doing. I tried Allison's number next. No answer there either. Where was everybody? I did leave a message for my daughter, saying that I loved her and would call back in a few hours to talk to her.

I donned my rain gear again and Buddy and I ran to the car under my big old umbrella. Buddy's shake was expected now and I just covered my face while he flung drops of water everywhere. Then we headed down the Notch Road for the second time today.

The difference in the road was amazing. I had a hard time distinguishing where the side of the road was. Water was everywhere and in motion. No puddling now. All the water was rushing down hill. I felt like I was driving in the river. I pumped my brakes gently, hoping they weren't too wet to slow me down. I needed those brakes for the sharp curves ahead. If they let go, I would plummet off the road and down into the deep ravines that the Notch Road passed through. Buddy sat up in the passenger seat and peered through the rain-smeared window. He whimpered a little as if he knew what a fix we were in.

"Calm down, Buddy," I said to him but was really trying to comfort myself. "If we take it slow and the brakes hold out we will be fine."

We were about half way down when the first big curve loomed through the pouring rain. I pumped my brakes and they didn't respond. I pumped harder. The car slowed a little, but not enough for me to make the curve without hydroplaning or skidding off into the drop below. I put my foot full down on the brake and at the same time down shifted into low and pulled on the emergency brake. The car slowed but fishtailed to the right as it hit deeper water near the side of the road. As the wheels hit the sandy shoulder, they sunk in enough to pull the car to a stop.

I sat there, just trying to breathe. My hands were gripping the wheel so hard I didn't think I could get them loose. Buddy whimpered again.

"It's OK, boy. We'll be fine." I wish I believed what I was saying. We were only half way down the hill and had several curvy dangerous miles to go before we reached the flats of the valley. And with all this water rushing down, I was afraid we would be riding into a flood when we got down there. What should I do?

Just as I was trying to decide whether to walk, turn the car around and try to get back home or continue down into town, a big black SUV came roaring around the curve on its way down the hill. It narrowly missed me as it took the turn too widely. I couldn't see any insignia on the outside of the vehicle and the windows were too tinted to see inside. The car never slowed down and continued on its way.

I was angry. Obviously, my car was half in the ditch which would indicate I needed some help. Anyone would know that I wasn't there to enjoy the view in the downpour and streaming road. Any person from town would have stopped to help me. So, the SUV couldn't have been from around here. I wondered who owned that car and thought of the description Josie had given of the black SUV she assumed was a police car on the night of Alice's death.

That thought did it. I started the car, carefully pulled back onto the road and followed the SUV down the hill. It helped having the SUV's red taillights signal when to brake. I just did what the other driver did and hoped he knew what he was doing. He pulled away from me, going faster than I wanted to go, but I kept him in sight, coming around a curve and spotting his lights as his car entered the next turn. It was a wild ride and I was exhausted from holding the steering wheel so tightly. Finally, we reached the bottom of Notch Road and forded the stream that filled the space where Notch Road crossed with Falls Road. The water was up to my fenders in some places and I prayed that my engine would keep going. Then the SUV sped ahead and I lost him on the road into the town center. I don't know where he pulled off. It was so hard to see up the side roads through the clouded and streaming wet windows while I was focusing on the road ahead and looking for dangerous spots. I gave up on finding him and drove to the library. As I crossed the stone bridge at the bottom of the falls, I was amazed to see the water so close. It was practically touching the bottom of the bridge and was hurtling along at a tremendous speed. I knew then that Hummingbird Falls had more trouble than just two deaths. Many people were now in danger of losing their livelihood and perhaps even their lives if the river spilled over its banks, flooding the town and taking buildings, houses and perhaps people with it.

Buddy and I ran through water several inches deep to the library door and rushed in dripping. At least it was warm in the library. I could see several space heaters going full blast. Pauline appeared from the stacks.

"I'm glad you got here safely. How are the roads?"

"Just awful. If the rain doesn't stop, we may not have any roads left at all. It's scary out there. Glad you have the heaters on. The rain has chilled everything down. I think the temperature is only in the low fifties right now."

"You might be right, but the heaters are more to keep down the dampness. The dehumidifiers aren't big enough to take care of all the moisture in here and the books are in danger of mold. It isn't just flooding that I worry about. Mold spores love this weather and love books, too. So I am trying to get as much dry air to the books as I can. You can help by opening up as many books as you can and that will let some air in. But first, help me move the books from the lower two shelves to the top shelves. They won't be in order, but at least if we flood in here, they won't be destroyed. I called all the members of the Library Committee, but they either can't make it here, or are sandbagging around their homes. The Walters already had to leave their house on the river and move into their son's house, which is on higher ground. I just don't know what we are going to do. It has to stop raining."

I started to reshelf the books Pauline pointed out to me. She was a stack away, doing the same thing. We didn't talk for a while, each of us in our own thoughts of how a flood would change this dear town.

After about an hour, Pauline asked me if I wanted to stop and have a cup of tea with her. I assured her I would love that and we made tea in the little back room and sat down waiting for it to steep in Pauline's clay pot.

"I usually eat my lunch here in bad weather, or take a quick break for tea. Sometimes I go over to the Little Church to sit quietly. But we don't need to talk about that. You said you had something to tell me. What is it?"

"Alice's will is going to be read tomorrow after her service and while the reception is going on at the Inn. All the beneficiaries must be present to hear the will. And, Pauline, you are one of the beneficiaries. Can you be there?"

"Me? Alice named me a beneficiary? Oh my goodness. What a shock. I never expected her to leave me anything. Especially after ..." Her voice died down. "Oh dear. Oh, my gosh! I am just in shock. Do you know what she left me?"

"No. I'm the executrix but I haven't heard the whole will yet. We will all find out tomorrow. Mr. Compton is reading the will."

"What about Colby? Is he a beneficiary?"

"I really can't disclose that yet, Pauline. Come to the reading and you will learn who all the beneficiaries are."

"Oh Alice," Pauline cried. "What have you done? What have you gone and done?"

"What are you talking about, Pauline? What has Alice done?"

"You didn't know Alice, Ellie, not really. There's more to her story than you or most people know about. I'm sure the Alice you knew was a wonderful friend, well educated and interesting, but there was another side to her."

"What other side? What are you saying?"

"I'm not saying anymore. You will probably find out tomorrow at the reading. Or if you don't, then maybe it is all for the good. Let the dead rest and take their secrets to the grave."

"Pauline, please tell me what you know. Alice and Josie are dead. If you know something that would help solve their murders then you have to speak up. Otherwise, you are an accomplice to the crime. What do you know?"

"I know enough to keep my mouth shut. I have already said too much, I'm sure. I don't want to be the next one on the list. And if you want to be safe, you better keep out of it, too. That's my advice to you."

I finished my tea in silence. She had repeated what Josie had told me almost word for word. I had hit a dead end with Pauline although I had learned quite a bit along the way, whether she knew it or not. I hoped when Dave interviewed her later this afternoon that he would find out more than I had.

"I have other people to call on, Pauline. So I'll be going. I'll try to spread the word that you need help moving the books. Will you be all right here by yourself?"

"Sure, Ellie. I'm a survivor. But any help you can send would be great. I'll see you at the service tomorrow, if not before. I'll be at the reading, too. My father lets me borrow his SUV when the weather's bad. I wouldn't miss the reading for anything."

I looked at the gleam in her eye and worried about what all I didn't know. I called Buddy and we ran back to our car and headed up the road to the Post Office to see Sarah.

The Post Office was empty. I called out, "Sarah, it's Ellie. Are you there?"

There was no answer. That was strange. The Post Office was open, but Sarah wasn't here. She would never leave the Post Office unlocked and unattended. I called again and when I received no answer I walked around the counter and into the main mailroom. Everything looked normal as far as I could see. I headed for the sorting room. The door to the little room was closed. I knocked softly. No answer. I turned the doorknob slowly. I had a bad feeling in my stomach. I almost didn't want to open the door.

Chapter 23

I COULDN'T OPEN the door very far. Something was blocking it. I stuck my head in as far as I could. Then I saw her. Sarah was lying on the floor. Her body kept the door from opening all the way.

"Oh no!" I screamed and pushed harder on the door, widening the space enough so I could slip through. I bent down and tried to feel for a pulse in Sarah's wrist. I thought I felt one. I put my face close to her nose and felt a wisp of breath. She wasn't dead, at least not yet.

I looked around and found the phone on the desk. I dialed 911 and urged them to send an ambulance as soon as possible. Then I called Dave and told him Sarah was hurt at the Post Office. He said he would be right over.

I sat with Sarah while I waited for help. I didn't see any sign of blood, but her face was pale and she wasn't making any sounds or movements. I was afraid for her. I tried to figure out what had happened to her. The sorting room was in order. A few envelopes were scattered on the floor and I noticed that Sarah held an envelope in her hand. She was probably sorting the mail when she fainted, had a stroke or experienced whatever had happened to her.

I eased the envelope out of her hand and glanced at it. It hadn't been postmarked, so it was a local letter waiting to go out, I assumed. I looked more closely. The envelope was addressed by hand, with dark black ink. It was intended for Dave, the chief of Police. And it had been opened.

My curiosity got the best of me and even while telling myself I shouldn't be doing this, I was unfolding the single page of paper and starting to read the black block letters that covered it.

"COLBY CONNERS IS THE KILLER. I KNOW THIS FOR A FACT.

YOU ARE WARNED. GET HIM OR I WILL."

I turned the paper over. It was blank. No other clue or explanation was given. Sarah had read the letter and then something happened to her. More mystery, which made no sense.

Finally, I heard the sirens approaching. The paramedics, followed by Dave, rushed in. They pushed me out of the tiny room. They went to work on Sarah. Dave started asking me questions and I answered him as well as I could. I handed him the letter I had found clutched in Sarah's hand. He scowled as he read it.

"What the hell is going on?" he asked while he reread the brief note again. This was in her hand? Any other mail in her hands?"

"No," I answered. "There is some scattered on the floor. What do you think the note means? Do you think Colby is really the killer?"

"No, I don't think Colby had anything to do with those two deaths. I think the killer wrote this note to throw us off, to distract us. But I don't understand how Sarah is involved in it. Why would she open mail addressed to me?"

"I have no idea. It's a federal crime, isn't it, to open someone's mail? Sarah wouldn't ever do that, would she? I mean, she's the Post Master."

"I don't believe she would open anyone's personal mail, ever. But I could be wrong. It sure looks like she opened this one. Maybe she has been reading everyone's mail all along. I wouldn't be surprised at anything with the way things are going around here. This is just crazy."

The chief paramedic stepped out of the sorting room and said, "Chief, we have to transport her to County Hospital right away. She is unconscious and nonresponsive. She seems to be in a deep coma. She has a large bump on the back of her head. Whether she was hit and fell or fell and then bumped her head, I'm not sure. She needs immediate care in case there is brain swelling or damage that could alter or stop her respiration or cardiac activity. Is it all right if we move her now?"

"Yes, go ahead. Just be careful on the roads. They are a slippery mess and we don't need you guys needing to be rescued too. Thanks. Tell the hospital I'll be checking in to find out her status. I want them to call me as soon as she becomes conscious and is able to talk."

The paramedics secured Sarah in a stretcher and covered her with a blanket and a plastic sheet to keep the rain from soaking her on the way out to the ambulance. I glanced at her as she passed by. She didn't look good. Her face looked pale white with black lines etched deeply in her skin. An oxygen mask covered her nose and mouth and an IV dangled from a tube taped to her arm.

Dave started examining the sorting room. "Doesn't look like any struggle took place. Everything is nice and tidy. If it weren't for this letter she was holding, I'd think Sarah just passed out or had a heart attack."

"That's what I thought too. What are you going to do now?"

"Well, I am scheduled to interview Pauline next. So, I have to get back to the office, write this up and continue with my interviews. Then I will head out to talk with Sarah when she is conscious. If she becomes conscious."

"Oh, don't say that, Dave. Of course, she'll regain consciousness. We can't have three deaths. It's just too much for us all. Sarah will be fine. She has to be. She'll explain why she opened this letter and what happened to her. At least, I hope so."

"My interview with Margaret and Mike weren't very productive. Margaret has an alibi for the time of both murders. She was with the art commune folks when Josie died and was out of town on a buying trip when Alice disappeared."

"But I saw her the very next morning, early, at the pastry shop."

"Yes, she said she just drove in to town and went right to the pastry shop and heard about the body in the falls. But she stayed the night at the Kensington Lodge in Edgertown. She has a receipt. I have to call and verify the names of people she said she was with, but it looks like she's in the clear. I didn't really think she was involved, but she did say she had been one of the last ones to see Alice."

"What about Mike?"

"No alibi. Just said he went home by himself after the meeting and watched TV the night Josie was killed. He did see Alice the night she disappeared. She had called him and asked him to come to her house and talk. He said Alice wanted him to put his land in a conservation easement to protect it. She argued that it wasn't fair for him to sell the land to developers because it was ruining their town. They had a big fight. Mike said he could do anything he wanted with his land and if he had to sell it to eat, then he would. I guess they parted on bad terms, but I don't think he would kill Alice, let alone Josie. He did say that Alice was really upset when he left. He noticed that she had quite a bit of wine to drink while he was there and might have been a little drunk. He didn't see James. Mike says he went right home after meeting with Alice and watched TV. Saw the 10:00 news. So we know Alice was alive at 10:00."

"If we believe Mike, you mean?"

"Yeah, if we believe Mike. But what would his motive be? I asked him if he had been romantically attached to Alice and he laughed. Said all they ever talked about was the town and the land."

"Well, I'm anxious to hear what you find out from Pauline. She knows a lot more than she's talking about. She and Colby have been involved in something that she feels guilty about and she said to me that she blames herself for someone's death. She started to tell me that Alice had some kind of secret life that not many people knew about, but then she shut up really quickly. She's scared, I think, and up to her ears in some intrigue. And now with that letter that says Colby's the killer, you better grill her good."

Dave chuckled. "Ellie, thanks for making me laugh, even at a time like this. You have a way with words. By the way, I don't 'grill'. I interview, interrogate. Cops have come a long way."

"You knew what I meant, Dave. But I'm glad you can laugh a little. Now what about the rain and the roads? There's nothing funny about that. I almost went off the Notch Road on my way down to town. And then, some obnoxious guy in a black SUV almost slammed into me. Didn't even check to see if I needed any help. What is this world coming to?"

"I don't know, Ellie. Did you get his license plate? I could run it for you and call him in for a talking to."

"Nope. I was too worried about falling down into the ravine at the time. Thanks though. If I see him again, I'll try for the plate."

"I'm asking everyone to stay off the roads unless it's an emergency, for tonight. The weather forecast says the rain should slow down tonight and stop by tomorrow, but you know how often weather forcasters are wrong. If we can just get through tonight, I think the bridges will hold, the roads will survive, or at least most of them, and we can avoid any horrendous flooding. But if we get any more major accumulation, we may have to call in the National Guard to help sandbag the river in spots and support the bridges. Keep you fingers crossed that this low moves out tonight."

"I sure will, Dave. I guess I'll try to make it back up the hill and contact the rest of the beneficiaries by phone. We aren't going to lose the power are we?"

"Probably will, Ellie. When the ground is so saturated, the trees lose root and start to fall. Then power lines are hit and the lights go out. Make sure you have candles and hurricane lamps. Listen to the radio. They will be announcing warnings all night."

"What about Alice's service?"

"Depends. We may have to cancel it. Can't tell yet. Larry lets me know what we can and can't do tonight and tomorrow. They are his roads. No one knows them any better."

"OK. I'll just pray for the rain to let up, and I'll pray for a few other things as well while I'm at it."

"Take care, Ellie. Go slow and you should be OK. Leave now before it gets dark so you have the best visibility you can get. Let's check in with each other tomorrow."

"Let me know about Sarah, if you can, Dave. I am worried about her."

"OK. I am just going to secure this building, call the feds about a postal replacement and get back to the office. You go on now."

I dreaded the ride up the mountain. Buddy welcomed me back into the car with lots of licks to my face and whiney love sounds. I responded with hugs and ear scratching. I drove over the stone bridge. The water looked like it had crept up a few more inches since I had been in town. The Notch Road was closed. A blockade of sawhorses prevented anyone from turning onto the road. I had to go miles out of my way now. I headed for the Cross Road, which would take me to Tinker Hill Road, which connected with Tanner Creek Road, which turned on to the far end of Durkin Farm Road. It certainly was the long way to go and in nice weather, it made for a beautiful ride. But I just wanted to get home now. With a sigh I turned onto the Cross Road and headed uphill, hoping I wouldn't run into any black SUVs or downhill rivers. I prayed for the rain to stop. And I prayed for some people and other things as well.

Chapter 24

IT ALL SEEMED to happen at the same time. The power went out with a crack. Buddy started to bark and jump up at the front windows and run to the front door, scratching to go out. And the back door slammed open in a gust of wind.

I didn't know which way to turn and couldn't see anything in the dark. I was totally disoriented. I stumbled my way toward the woodstove and grappled for the matches I kept on the shelf. Where was the flashlight? I found my nail clippers, a small earthen pot, one of Buddy's treats. My hand closed around the box of matches. Now I just had to find the candle and I would have light.

Buddy had stopped barking and was now growling deep in his throat. The hair on the back of my neck rose. From the sound of his growl he was moving closer to me. I reached a hand out and whispered. "Buddy, come here, boy."

I felt the fur on his back stiffen as he moved next to my leg. I grabbed hold of his collar. He was trembling with tension and strained toward the kitchen in the back of the house. I heard the back door slamming in the wind and then the crash of glass breaking.

"Who's there?" I called out. There was no answer, but I heard heavy footsteps crunching on broken glass. Where was the phone? I had to call for help. Someone was in my kitchen and the only protection I had was Buddy.

"I have a big dog here. He's trained to attack on command. If you don't leave immediately, I'll release him and command him to attack." I was bluffing, but I hoped it would work.

The noise of furniture being knocked about in the kitchen, coupled with an angry sounding guttural expression filled the dark air. What was going on? Holding on to Buddy's collar, and trying not to stumble over any furniture, I quietly moved toward the phone table. I picked up the phone and punched what I thought was 911. Nothing. The phone was dead. I tried it again and again. It definitely was not working. Now what?

Clashing and banging continued in the kitchen. It sounded like someone was trashing the room. I opened the drawer in the table and fumbled around trying to find something to use as a weapon. I felt a cylindrical metal form. A flashlight. I remembered now I had put flashlights in several places just in case the cottage lost power. I had a source of light in my hand.

I turned the flashlight on and moved closer to the kitchen and eased open the door. I flashed the light around the room. Suddenly two of the biggest black eyes I had ever seen gleamed straight at me, caught in the light. I slowly lowered the beam of light from the eyes, to the face and then on down the body. Then I froze with fear. Standing in my kitchen staring at me was a huge dripping wet black bear, with blueberry turnovers filling his mouth and covering a great deal of his chin. I screamed and lost hold of Buddy's collar. Buddy dashed into the kitchen, barking loudly.

A wild scene of chaos erupted. I only caught pieces of the action as I moved the flashlight here and there trying to see what was happening. I screamed Buddy's name again and again, but he was so involved with chasing the bear around the kitchen table that he ignored me. Finally, the bear stood his ground, rising up and growling. Fast as lightning, he lunged at Buddy, slashing his clawed front paw out at him. Buddy jumped back out of reach, barking and growling. The back door slammed open again in the wind. The bear took his chance and fled out the open back door and right through the ripped screen door into the pouring rain. Another gust of wind slammed the door closed after him. I rushed over and locked the door. Buddy was frantic to pursue the bear. He whined and barked, scratched at the back door and ran around the cottage sniffing until I told him to quiet down. I shut the door to the kitchen so he wouldn't hurt himself in the broken glass and then I made sure the other doors and windows were locked. I walked back to the kitchen and surveyed the damage with my flashlight.

Instantly, I spotted the reason the bear had intruded. I had left the back door unlocked and the wind had blown it open. Only the screen door blocked the bear from the luscious smells emanating from the kitchen. The screen door was no match for a hungry bear's front claws.

The box of freshly baked blueberry turnovers I had purchased in the village just before I came up the hill was smashed and chewed up. The sugar bowl was turned over and wet sugar was all over the floor, mixed with honey from the honey pot I left on the kitchen table so I could spread it on my toast in the morning. Frosted Flakes spilled out the ripped box and dotted the wet muddy floor like new snow. All this sticky mess was mixed up with broken chairs, Buddy's bag of kibbles, broken china and glasses and assorted other kitchen implements and food that had somehow fallen during the fray. What a mess.

Well, now I had another bear story. One I didn't really want to have. I decided that there was no sense trying to clean up before the lights came back on. I closed the door on the bedlam and I used my flashlight to find the candles and hurricane lights and before long I had the living room looking as cozy as could be. I sat down and checked Buddy's paws. The cut on his back paw that the vet had attended to looked fine. There was a little blood on his left front paw that I cleaned up and washed, but it didn't look too serious. I gave Buddy his antibiotics and wished I had a miracle drug to take as well. I put another log in the wood stove and sat down and tried to figure out what I should do.

No phone. No electricity. It was a good thing I had called the other beneficiaries to inform them of the meeting tomorrow after Alice's service before I lost phone service. I had also called Larry and talked briefly with his wife who said she didn't expect him back until the weather cleared up. That could be days. I left a message with her for Larry, saying I was looking for a rod iron stake or hanger. She said he hadn't had much time to forge any lately and that for the last several months he had been too busy to sell out of his garage as he usually did in the summer. He had taken his entire inventory to Heppie's flower shop. I also found out that the only forged iron rods in town now were Larry's as he had signed a non-compete clause with all the gift stores in town. That meant if one of Larry's rods was found to be the murder weapon there was a good chance we could trace who had bought the rod.

That perked me up a bit until I remembered that I couldn't reach my kids, either, and they couldn't get through to me. I would just have to wait until tomorrow. What else could I do?

I had no portable radio so I couldn't find out the weather forecast. I didn't even know if Alice's service would be held or cancelled. All I did know was that it was still raining, a bear had attacked my kitchen, Buddy had saved my life, and we both were alive and very alone in the dark on Durkin Farm Road.

Buddy and I curled up on the couch. I wanted to go to bed, but I didn't want to blow out the candles and leave the whole cottage in darkness. I was too scared for that. What if the bear tried to get in again? I decided we would just stretch out on the couch and nap. When the lights came on, we would go into the bedroom and really sleep.

Suddenly the room was filled with lights. Car doors were slamming and men's voices were yelling. Buddy started barking. I jumped up and looked out the window. There must have been five or six cars and trucks parked on my front lawn with their headlights on high shining into my front windows. A crowd of rain gear covered males was headed for my porch.

I was unsure of what to do until I recognized Mike Greeley's voice calling, "Ellie, Ellie, are you in there?"

I grabbed my flashlight and opened the door. Mike Greeley, Herb Anderson, and several other men I knew by sight were standing in the pouring rain.

"Come in, come in," I called. "Don't stand out there getting all wet."

They trooped up onto the porch. Their headlights spotlighted us all as if we were on a stage. My little flashlight was practically useless in the halogen bombardment.

"What's wrong? Why are you here? What has happened?" I asked.

Chapter 25

"WE HAVE BEEN deputized by Dave to help during this emergency. We are charged with evacuating the citizens of Hummingbird Falls to a safer site. Dave is too busy with the investigation of the murders and Larry is too tied up trying to save the bridges. So they have called us in to help."

"What are you doing?" I asked.

"We are riding the roads, where they still open, at least, and checking up on everyone. We can offer you shelter where you will be safer. The Little Church is opening its doors, at least temporarily, to take in people who have to be evacuated because of high water, flooding or road closings. Chuck said he would take any people who are living alone and want to stay closer to other people, for safety's sake. Of course, if the river floods the town, then everyone at the Church shelter will have to be evacuated to higher ground. I advise you to pack a bag now and one of us will take you down to the church."

"I don't know if I want to do that. I feel safe enough here, I think. I'm not in danger of being flooded out. I'm up too high for that. I'm sure the lights will be on soon. Right now my biggest worry is the bear that just broke in and trashed my kitchen."

"We passed a big black bear down the road," said Herb. "Could be that was your bear. Did he do any damage?"

"See for yourself," I said as I opened the door and waved them in.

They all trooped into the kitchen with flashlights blazing and oohed and ahhed over the mess in the kitchen. They seemed to think it was quite a humorous event.

"Well, Ellie. You have a good bear story now. Only story better would be if the bear swiped at you and caused an observable wound. Now that would be a number one bear story, but this one is pretty good."

Mike said, "Better just leave this mess. It isn't going anywhere. But I advise you to come with us. You just aren't safe up here by yourself until the power is on and the roads are safe. And I don't believe the power will be on for days. Lots of the poles are down. Wires are all over the place. It's dangerous out there. It would be terrible if something happened to you just because you were too stubborn to go to the shelter."

"I don't feel like I'm being stubborn, Mike. And I'm not alone. I have Buddy here with me. He saved me from the bear and I won't leave him here. Is Chuck allowing pets in the church?"

Herb said, "Ellie, you know Chuck. He wouldn't turn anyone or anything away. I'm sure you can take your dog with you. You have to take this more seriously. You have to think about the flooding and the roads, too. You could get cut off up here if the roads get any worse. The wash outs are everywhere now and driving is hazardous. If you get stuck up here, it could be weeks before you can get power or drive down to town. What if you got sick or needed something? Larry told us to warn everyone about the road conditions and asked us to help him monitor the roads while we were out riding around. I've never seen the roads so bad."

"We all have big four wheel drive SUVs that can go off road if necessary. I don't think your Subaru can do that. Ellie, come with us." Mike was getting more insistent.

"I could pull rank and make you come," he threatened.

"I don't think you would do that, would you?" I answered.

"I would have to, Ellie. It might be too late if you decide you want to evacuate tomorrow. We may not be able make it up here to take you down, if you stayed and the weather conditions got worse. Right now we are here and can help you. It just makes sense given the road conditions and the need for safety."

I gave in. I really wanted to stay put in my own place. I wasn't exactly afraid to stay by myself with Buddy and I was sure that the flooding wouldn't affect me because I was up so high. I was more bothered by the fact that power might not be restored and that I could be isolated for an indefinite period of time before the roads were safe enough to travel. How could I exist without food, and especially without my turnover fix? And I didn't want to miss Alice's service. I had to be there for the reading of the will. I gave in.

"OK, I'll come with you, but you have to wait for me to pack a bag. I have to have the right clothes for Alice's funeral service tomorrow morning."

"Oh, I forgot to tell you. Larry has cancelled all meetings, ordered the downtown shops closed and all roads into the town closed down due to the potential danger of flooding. He told me that Alice's service is cancelled. He doesn't want a lot of people driving and anyway the Little Church is being used as a shelter. He put all the cancellation notices on the radio station."

"I don't have a wireless radio, so I didn't know. Well, I still have to pack a bag. It will only take a minute."

I quickly gathered a duffle bag full of clothes, threw in my toiletries and a book, and looked around to see if there was something else I needed to take. Just Buddy's pills and food. I was ready.

"You go with Herb, Ellie. The rest of us will continue driving around to the other homes up here in the hills, warning them and helping them to come into town now while they still can. I hope they aren't as stubborn as you."

Buddy and I climbed up into Herb's oversized SUV.

"Boy, we are up high," I said.

"Better visibility and higher frame so the water is less apt to short out the electrical system and we can go through the rougher sections without so much risk. These big boys take a lot of gas, but you can't beat them in the snow or in emergencies like this. Buckle up good. This will be a wild ride."

I buckled up and held Buddy tightly. Herb was right. The ride down the mountain was more than wild. It was terrifying. In some places there was no road at all. The asphalt was gone, replaced with sandy ditches, some more than four feet deep. Herb would ease the big vehicle down and then gun it up and out. Buddy would be barking and I would be gasping for breath. In other sections, big fissures had formed and we would have to creep around them, hoping they would hold up long enough for us to pass. Once a tree across the road blocked our way. Herb stopped and got a chain saw out of the back and sawed us a way through. Since I had driven up the mountain the whole terrain had changed. Now the roads looked like an earthquake had hit them. I would never have been able to make it down on my own.

"Thanks Herb," I said as we bumped over the trunk of a small birch that was lying in the road. I'm sorry I made such a fuss back there. I had no idea the roads were this bad. I wouldn't have made it in my car."

"If it makes you feel any better, the roads weren't this bad when we came up. I'm amazed at how fast they are crumbling. Larry must be having a fit. This is a disaster. Going to take big equipment to put everything to rights again."

We were quiet on the rest of the ride down. When we drove into town, I noticed a group of people by the stone bridge. Herb stopped before the bridge and we got out to see what was happening.

"Hi there," Larry called. "We can use all the help we can get. We are sandbagging the footings at the edge of the bridge. The water is up so high, we are going to lose her in the next few hours if we don't build up a barrier around the supports."

While I shoveled sand into burlap bags with a couple of other rain geared folks, Larry, Herb and about a dozen others loaded them into a bull dozer bucket and hauled them down the slope to barricade the footing of the bridge. After a couple of back breaking hours, we realized we were fighting a losing battle.

Larry called us together. "You did a great job. Thanks. But I'm afraid the river has us beat. We can't stop it or detour it enough to keep pressure off the footings. We are just going to have to pray. And we are going to have to evacuate everyone in town who could be in danger of flooding. We'll use the fire engines and town trucks and take everyone up to the Inn on the Hill. The Inn isn't very far out of town, but it is high enough to be safe from flooding. They have a big generator so their water, lights, plumbing are still working. They have enough room to put everyone up there, on the floors if necessary. I could use some help in alerting everyone."

Larry assigned each person to an area to cover. He asked me to go to the shelter in The Little Church and help get them organized to move within the next hour. Buddy and I walked to the church and opened the door. Dozens of burning candles created a cozy atmosphere and provided enough light to see by. I was surprised that most of the pews were filled with people, blankets, bags of clothing and baskets of food. Children and animals were chasing each other up and down the aisles. If I didn't know better, I would have thought the ladies of the church were throwing a big indoor picnic.

I made my way to Chuck who was talking to the food table ladies while trying to assign a family to a pew area with enough room to hold them all.

"Excuse me, Chuck, but I just talked with Larry. He says we all have to get ready to move to higher ground. The Little Church is in the potential flood area. Within the hour we will be transported to The Inn on the Hill. They have enough food and room for everyone and it will be more comfortable than church pews. They even have generated power."

"I'm glad to hear that, Ellie. We are just about full up and I hear they are bringing more people down from the hills. I'll make the announcement and get everyone packing."

Just then Dave came into the church. He looked ten years older and very weary.

"Folks, listen up. Thanks for your attention. I know you have had a hard time, but the weather is not cooperating with us and things are getting worse, not better. We are in a state of disaster. The Governor declared this whole area eligible for federal help in the last hour. That means the Red Cross and other groups such as FEMA will be able to assist us. But they have to reach us first. For now, it is up to us to keep safe and sound. Fortunately, The Inn on the Hill has agreed to take everyone in. We will start the evacuation immediately. As soon as you are ready, move to the door. As a vehicle pulls up, climb in, as many as will fit. Next in line take the next and so forth. It will take a while, but we will get you all to safety. Don't worry. No one will be left behind. Every home is being evacuated and everyone is ordered to go to the Inn. There are no exceptions. Those up high in the hills are being brought down as the roads are virtually impassable now and will be out of commission for an indeterminate length of time. Without power up there some folks would have a rough go of it for what could be a really extended period of time. So, we are in a bit of a mess right now. Don't lose courage; we will get through this fine, if we all stick together, help one another and keep our spirits up."

People began to gather up their things and call children and dogs to join them. The church ladies wrapped food and covered bowls and casseroles. Chuck stood by the door to keep the line moving and to offer prayers and encouragement to the tired crowd.

I moved over to Dave and waited until he had finished a conversation with an elderly gentleman worried about his home.

"We will continue patrolling the roads all around town, Mr. Siles. No looting will be allowed. Anyway, everyone will be evacuated. No one will be allowed to stay in this area. Your home will be safe from burglars. I can't promise that it will be safe from flood damage, but I can guarantee that no one will be breaking into it."

Dave turned to me. "Ellie, they dragged you down here I see. I'm glad you came. Can you talk to me for a minute? Let's go into Chuck's office. It will be more private."

I followed Dave into Chuck's office and shut the door.

"What is it, Dave?" I asked.

"Sarah still hasn't gained consciousness. She has a severe concussion. They expect her to survive, but have no idea when she will wake up, or if she will wake up."

"Oh no. Poor Sarah. I feel so badly for her. She must have seen who did this to her. If we could only talk to her."

"We can't. So, we have to find other ways. This damn weather and flood possibility has really prevented me from doing much on finding out who killed Alice and Josie. Some people are starting to act out their anger. I've had several calls asking me to resign and let the State Police take over the case. Maybe I should. I just don't know. There's so much going on."

"The State Police couldn't do any more right now than you are doing, Dave. You can't stop Mother Nature and the rain isn't your fault. Let's stick to what we know. How did the interview with Pauline go?"

"Fine. She's really upset about Alice, Josie and Sarah. She saw Alice the day before she went missing. She said Alice asked her to come over and talk. Pauline arrived at Alice's right after she left the library at 5:00pm. They had a couple of drinks and a nice talk and then Pauline left around 6:30pm. She thought she saw Mike's Subaru turning into the driveway as she drove away. That checks out with Mike's alibi. Pauline was at the town meeting the night Josie was killed. She said she left a little early because her father wasn't feeling very well. She was working when Sarah was hurt. You said you came from the library and Pauline was there right before you found Sarah."

"That's right. Pauline was shelving books when I left, so she couldn't have done anything to Sarah, unless Sarah had been lying there for over two hours. Is that possible?"

"I don't know how long Sarah was unconscious. Probably no one came to the post office that day. It was raining so hard. She could have been there for several hours and no one would have known."

"Oh now, I remember. I called the Post Office before I headed down to town and there wasn't any answer. I thought it was strange at the time. Maybe Sarah had already been hurt before I called. Did Pauline say anything about Colby?"

"She said that their relationship was a thing of the past and that she's no longer interested in him. He's the one pursuing her, according to her. I have heard differently from Colby, so that story doesn't add up. So, I really didn't get much from her. The other people who saw Alice didn't add anything either. The delivery boy from Reggie's just gave her the groceries and said he didn't notice anything strange. Two people who talked to her on the phone said nothing was amiss. Alice was just as she always was. And Heppie said Alice came in two days before she went missing to buy some things for the garden and was most pleasant."

"What did she buy?"

"I didn't ask. Oh damn. Maybe she bought the rod iron pole from Heppie. Is that what you were getting at?"

"Yep. Exactly. If she bought the pole then it was available to whoever killed her."

"I'll talk to Heppie again. I don't know what's wrong with me. I keep missing things."

"Dave, give yourself a break. You have a lot on your mind. You have the responsibility with Larry of the whole town in your hands. Of course, a few things will slip by. Let me talk to Heppie. I'll see her up at the Inn on the Hill. In fact, I'll talk to Pauline again. We had started a conversation that we never finished."

"I called James Foster to ask him some follow up questions and he never answered the phone. I doubt he'll be at the Inn on the Hill because Alice's house is out of danger. I don't think anyone could drag him down to stay with all of us at the Inn, even if we ordered him. I don't think he feels he belongs here anymore."

"Make him be there, Dave. Force him to evacuate like everyone else. Tell him it's some state order or decree. Put the pressure on him. In close quarters with everyone in town, he might start sweating a bit and maybe he will make some mistakes and let something out."

"Good idea, Ellie. I'll send Herb and Colby over to get him. Then you can observe him at the Inn. I'm willing to try anything right about now."

We parted. Dave went on with his rescue effort and Buddy and I stuffed ourselves in someone's minivan and rode up to the Inn on the Hill with a group of other shelter people. The road to the Inn was in fairly good shape so we didn't have any trouble, but the rain was relentless, pouring down on the homeless from Hummingbird Falls as we flowed into the lobby of the Inn, discouraged, dripping and despondent. Even Buddy kept his tail between his legs and his ears drooping down.

Chapter 26

THE HUGE GATHERING of people was quiet and obedient as one by one or family-by-family they were assigned areas in the Inn. Cots had been set up everywhere. Signs were posted with arrows pointing out bathrooms, food tables, and registration. Missing person's bulletins cluttered the walls. The Inn had been transformed from a four star hotel to an emergency facility.

Faces reflected fear, worry, anxiety, and depression. Eyes held questions about the survival of homes, shops, friends and relatives and about the future of the town of Hummingbird Falls itself. What would tomorrow bring? Although few of the residents of Hummingbird Falls had ever experienced the grandeur of the Inn on the Hill before, unless they worked there, the luxurious details failed to interest them. Their minds and hearts were elsewhere.

I spotted Pauline in a corner, talking with Bonnie and her family. I made my way to them and settled Buddy down on his blanket with a treat.

"How are you guys doing?" I asked.

"I am so worried about the library," Pauline said. "I am so afraid we will lose our books, let alone our building. What will I do then?"

Bonnie tried to consol her, but Pauline obsessed over the possible loss of her job and her future. She showed little concern about the others who were at risk of losing as much or more than she was. I was surprised at her demeanor. I asked Bonnie to find some coffee for Pauline and she left, looking rather relieved.

"Pauline, have you seen James Foster?"

She looked sharply at me. "Why would I have seen him? He and I don't run in the same circles."

"I just wondered if he was here, at the Inn."

"I wouldn't know that. I don't keep tabs on James Foster."

"If you do see him, tell him I am looking for him, will you?"

"Sure, Ellie. You certainly have become really involved with us all, haven't you? For an outsider, you are nosing right into our business. Why don't you let Dave handle the investigation? What are you up to anyway?"

I was shocked at Pauline's personal attack. Usually, she was so quiet, so reserved. I had seen her crying and sad, but never like this. Perhaps she was so angry about what was happening to her town that she was displacing her feelings onto me. I decided to overlook her insulting words.

"Pauline, I am not up to anything. I just want to help, that's all. Things just keep happening where I am and that's how I seem to be in the middle of the investigation. But I'm as confused as you are."

"I'm not confused, Ellie. Maybe you are. Maybe Dave is. But I know what is going on."

"What?" I looked around to see if anyone was eavesdropping. Not surprising, almost everyone else was either asleep, going by the food table, or talking in small groups. James Foster didn't seem to be among them.

"You said that before Pauline, when I was at the library. And you mentioned that you knew something even earlier at the Little Church the other day. What are you hinting at? What do you know, Pauline?"

She leaned closer to me. "I'm going to tell you what I know, so you can tell Dave. I know that Colby is involved in this up to his neck."

"Colby?" I asked. "What does he have to do with Alice, Josie and Sarah?"

"Colby was at Alice's house the night of her murder."

"How do you know this?"

"When I left Alice's, I thought I saw another car coming down the hill, so I pulled over and turned out my car lights and watched. It was Mike's truck, I'm pretty sure. I left and drove toward town. About half way down the Notch Road I met Colby coming up. We stopped and talked for a minute. I asked him if he were going to see Alice. We had a fight about that earlier this month. I didn't want him hanging all over Alice."

"What did he say?"

"He told me it was none of my business and we got into it again. He said he would see Alice when he wanted to and he didn't want to hear any lectures from me. We both went our ways. But a little later, around nine thirty, my curiosity got the best of me and I drove to Alice's and Colby's car was there."

"Was Mike there, too?"

"No, Mike must have left earlier. I didn't see his car. But Colby was there. I saw his car. He must have killed Alice."

"Why are you telling me this, Pauline? I thought you and Colby were pretty tight. Now, you are accusing him of murder. And why tell me when you think it's none of my business? Why don't you tell Dave?"

"Dave won't listen to me. I try to tell him things and he just ignores me. He's been protecting Colby for years. He covers for him when he makes mistakes and does his work for him when Colby slacks off. He would never believe that Colby would kill Alice. Maybe since you're nosing around anyway and obviously reporting to Dave, you could convince him to look at Colby more truthfully and with less bias."

"Why do you believe Colby is the murderer, Pauline? How can you think such a thing?"

"I know Colby better than anyone. I know how deeply his resentment and rage are hidden and how it can pop out when he's triggered. He used to go into rages when we were together. Once he even beat me up. That's why we split up."

Pauline's version of events was contrary to what I had learned from others, and I wondered whom I should believe. Why was she telling me this? I had a hard time believing she was just ready to open up and spill everything out. I suspected she had an agenda. Revenge? Anger at Colby over his attention to Alice?

"What about Josie, Pauline? Why would Colby kill Josie?"

"She saw him, I think. She runs around at night. Everyone knows that. I think she saw him kill Alice and dump her in the falls."

"But he was at the town meeting the night Josie died. I saw him and you in the back."

"Then he left to search for her. He had plenty of time to get to her house and kill her."

"And Sarah? Why would he try to kill Sarah?"

"Because of the letter she opened which accused Colby. Maybe he didn't want to kill anyone, but had to keep on because one thing led to another. Oh I don't know. I tried so hard to keep him out of trouble, to keep him away from Alice and now look at the trouble he is in. I will never forgive myself."

Pauline broke down in tears before I could ask her how she knew about the letter that Sarah had clutched in her hand as she lay unconscious on the Post Office floor. I sat beside Pauline while she wept and tried to fathom what she had told me. Colby was the murderer. My first instinct had been to suspect Colby and now Pauline was confirming my suspicions. I had to find Dave and fast. I excused myself when Bonnie returned with coffee for Pauline and I hugged Pauline goodbye.

146

"I'll do what I can to help," I told her as I woke Buddy and gathered his blanket.

The women at the food table looked worn and weary, but greeted Buddy and me with a smile and an offer of food. For once, I turned them down and asked if they had seen Dave.

"Not for a few minutes. He walked outside a while ago with Larry and Colby, I think," said Jennie, who was in charge of the table.

I headed for the door. Outside the rain was still coming down in sheets. I walked back to the food table and asked Jennie if she would watch Buddy for a few minutes while I looked for Dave. I didn't want Buddy to get all dripping wet again. She was delighted and sat right down on the floor next to him.

As I went out the door, I turned and saw Jennie feeding Buddy oatmeal cookies. He was very happy, tail wagging and eyes sparkling. He didn't seem to miss me at all.

No one was on the wide front porch, so I put up my umbrella and walked down to the parking lot, which was off to one side of the Inn. Without any lights, it was hard to see my way. Evidently, the generator just powered inside utilities. I walked down the row of cars, looking for the big police patrol SUV or signs of men talking together. I saw neither.

Suddenly, I felt a sharp pain explode in my brain. Red and white light streamed through my eyes as I sunk to the ground, helpless. Just before I lost consciousness I saw a pair of rubber boots standing by my head. I told myself to remember the boots and that was the last thing I was aware of.

Chapter 27

MY HEAD HURT so much I didn't dare to open my eyes. The pain was so severe I was afraid I was going to throw up. A throbbing beat drummed along the top of my skull and pulsed in my ears. Warm liquid was trickling down my neck. I thought at first I must be out in the rain, but soon I realized rain would be cold and this liquid was warm. I was bleeding from a wound to my head.

I was relieved that I could think logically. At least I wasn't unconscious, or delirious. I decided to try to open my eyes.

I was blind. I couldn't see anything. Everything was black. I shut my eyes again. Black. I tried opening my eyes again. Nothing. I couldn't even see shadows or shades of light. My chest heaved and my sightless eyes filled with tears. I could bear the pain of the injury, but I couldn't stand to live if I were blind.

Slowly I tried to turn my head. It hurt to move, but I could twist my neck and head from side to side if I moved very slowly. If I moved too swiftly, I felt nauseous. I couldn't see no matter which way I turned. I lay still for a moment and tried to think what to do.

I tried to wipe my eyes, but discovered that my hands were taped behind me. My feet were taped together. But my body was free to roll over and I could get on my knees and hobble. Instantly, I bumped into a wall and fell back on my taped arms with my knees bent under me. I cried out with pain. Carefully I got myself straightened around again and lay panting on the floor. I inched toward the wall and pushed myself up to a sitting position and leaned against it.

My activity had caused the blood to flow more strongly through my hair and down the back of my neck. My shirt was soaked. I felt woozy. Had I lost too much blood to survive? I moaned my despair.

I sat against the wall for what seemed like hours, but was probably only minutes. The dripping blood slowed and then stopped. As long as I didn't move too quickly, perhaps the blood would coagulate around the wound. I decided to stay still for a while longer.

I remembered that people who lose one sense often compensate by becoming more dependent on their other senses. I listened as hard as I could in spite of the throbbing that continued to pound in my ears. I couldn't hear anything at all. Not a whisper of sound. I tried banging my feet on the floor. Thank goodness, I heard that. I snapped my fingers. I called out, I hummed. I could hear. I could speak. I could yell. And I started to yell, trying to hold my head still at the same time so

I wouldn't get sick or start the wound bleeding again. I yelled and yelled. And then I listened. I was the only sound there was. It was as if my voice just disappeared into the blackness. More frightening, it was like I was the only one left in the world. I started to cry. I didn't know what else I could do. I was afraid I would never see the people I loved again and I didn't want to die. I had too much living to do.

After a few minutes of crying, I didn't feel any better, so I thought about what else I could do. I decided to start inching my way around the room, keeping the wall at my back. I came to a corner. The walls were cool, rough like concrete. I continued down the next wall and to the next corner. No doors, no openings that I could feel. I inched my way along the third wall with the same results. There had to be a door somewhere. But it wasn't on the fourth wall either. What kind of place was I in?

I tried inching slowly across the floor, feeling for a trap door. I didn't find anything. Just the smooth, cool concrete. That meant the door had to be in the ceiling of my cell. I would have to stand up and try to hop around searching for it. But with my hands tightly taped behind me, how was I to reach up to feel for it? I had to get my hands free. That was all there was to it. I worked my hands back and forth against the layers of tape that held them together. There was almost no give at all. I stretched my fingers as far as I could hoping I could shred the tape with my nails. I got nowhere.

I tried to remember all the scenes in movies where someone was duct taped and how they escaped. In one escape the heroine managed to pull her arms under her butt and over her legs, so her hands were in front of her and then she bit the tape apart. Of course, the actress was a size 2 and the film was probably edited so it appeared that she accomplished the feat, but it was worth a try.

I bent forward as far as I could and sat on my hands. The pain in my arms increased until I couldn't bear it any longer. I lay on my side and bent up my knees in front and tried to pull my arms under my butt that way. No way were my tightly bound wrists going to make it around my turnover-fattened bum. I tried everyway I could manage and finally had to give up. I lay panting on the floor and cursing Hollywood special effects and all double-jointed gymnasts.

I tried yelling again and got nowhere. I tried rubbing the tape against the concrete wall and only succeeded in causing abrasions up and down my arms. I tried reaching my feet with my mouth to bite the tape off. My middle blocked that effort. No matter what I tried, I couldn't even loosen the tape. I felt helpless.

Then I heard something. A very faint creak sounded like it came from over head. I yelled and yelled. Then I listened. Nothing. Maybe I imagined the noise. Maybe I was trapped here until I died. Suddenly I became furious. I wasn't going to die in a hole like a rat. I pushed myself to my feet. I jumped up as high as I could and landed flat on my face. I heard a bone crack and blood poured out of my nose. I lost consciousness again.

Chapter 28

I WAS SO thirsty when I woke up. My tongue was glued to the roof of my mouth. Crusts of drying blood coated my nose, mouth and chin. I checked out my teeth with my tongue. None were missing or loose. I sent gratitude for that favor upward and prayed for help. I looked blindly upwards as I prayed and all of a sudden stopped. I could see a small dot of light. I blinked. Yes, there it was. Like a star in the midnight sky I saw a piece of light overhead. I wasn't blind. I could see. Tears washed down my bloody face.

I focused on the spot of light. Then I heard a scratching noise above me. Voices joined the scratching sound. I yelled.

"I'm here. I'm down here. Help me. Help."

A faint male voice said, "Hold on. We're here. We will get you out. Is it you, Ellie?"

"Yes," I yelled with relief. "It's me. Help me please. I'm hurt."

Dave's voice called down, "We just have to break the padlock open. You'll hear a loud noise, so don't get worried."

"Just do whatever you have to. Get me out of here, Dave. Oh my gosh. I'm so glad you're here."

Just then a loud metal clash on metal drowned out Dave's answer. With a screech and a ripping sound a large square hole of light appeared in the ceiling.

"What the hell?" Dave grunted as he bent over the trap door and looked down. "Quick, guys, get a ladder or a rope. Let's get her out of here."

It only took a few minutes to lower the ladder. Dave climbed down and with his pocketknife sliced the tape from my ankles and wrists. He lifted me up and called for help from above.

"I'm bringing her up a few steps. You guys reach down and grab her and we'll hoist her out. Be careful now. She's hurt."

In no time I was up and out lying on a stretcher in the wine cellar of the Inn on the Hill. Buddy licked my face and tried to climb on top of me. The only lights were from the flashlights of my rescuers, Dave, Herb, Mike and a man who managed the Inn.

"Easy boy," said Herb as he pulled Buddy off me and held him by his collar to prevent him from jumping on me again.

"How did you find me?" I asked.

"We didn't. Buddy did. When you didn't return to get Buddy from Jenny, she was worried and called me. We sent out a search party, but you had just disappeared into thin air. When we went back inside to check with anyone who might have seen you, Buddy escaped and ran out the door. We followed him to the parking lot and then around the back of the Inn. He scratched at the back door and it was unlocked so we went in. We found the manager and he said the steps went down to the basement. We came down and searched everywhere, but didn't find any sign of you. We were just about to give up when Buddy started to dig up a scatter rug that lay between the rows of wine in the wine cellar section of the basement. We pulled up the rug and found the trap door. It was metal and padlocked. Then we heard you. Buddy went wild. We broke the lock and you know the rest. Now tell us what happened to you."

"I wish I knew. I was out in the parking lot looking for you, Dave, to tell you something important that I found out. I can't remember what it was now, but I know it was important. Anyway, I felt this crack to the back of my head and dropped like a rock. When I woke up I was in the hole. It was totally dark. I thought I had gone blind."

I started to cry again and Dave patted me on the shoulder. "We are going to carry you upstairs now and get you tended to. That looks like a bad bump on your head and you've lost a lot of blood, judging by your clothes. Your nose is swollen, too. We will have to check if it is broken. Any other injuries that we should know about? Any pain?"

"My head feels like it has been mashed. I have a whale of a headache. My face hurts and my arms are stinging from rubbing them against the concrete wall. Other than that, I think I'm all right. Thank you for saving me. I was afraid no one would ever find me. I guess that was the intention of whoever tried to put me out of commission."

"Anything else you can remember would help a lot, Ellie," Dave said as four men lifted the stretcher I was on and started up the steps.

"Just the boots," I said. "The black rubber boots." I looked at Dave. "They were just like yours."

Chapter 29

MY NOSE WASN'T broken, but it took twelve stitches to close the gash on my head. My head felt like a smashed pumpkin and hurt like hell. I didn't want to take the painkillers offered by those who were serving as the medical staff because I wasn't feeling safe and wanted to be as alert as possible in case my attacker decided to try again. But I relented and was relieved to find that they kicked in pretty fast. Buddy wouldn't leave my side and I wouldn't have let him if he tried. People swarmed around Buddy and me like we movie stars. Buddy loved the attention as much as I hated it. Finally, the nurse who was attending me told the crowd that I needed to rest and they moved away. We were finally left alone. The nurse helped me to my assigned cot, in one corner of the Inn's large dining room, which had been converted to the women's dormitory. The only light was an emergency spotlight mounted in one corner of the room. Buddy lay next to me and before long my eyes were closing and I was nodding into dreamland.

"Ellie, are you awake? Ellie, wake up."

The voice caught me just as I was beginning to dream about the pastry shop and a table full of blueberry turnovers. I hadn't even had a bite before I was awakened.

"What is it?" I mumbled as I turned over to face the speaker.

"I need to talk with you, right now," whispered Colby.

"What are you doing in the women's dorm?" I asked. "This is off limits to men."

"I have to talk to you. It's very important," said Colby.

I sat up and a wave of dizziness swept over me. "Hold on a second, Colby. I'm still feeling some of the effects of the painkillers and that blow on my head. You'll have to wait. I'm feeling really sick right now."

Colby sat down on the edge of my bed. I leaned against the wall and waited for my vertigo to ease.

"What do you want, Colby?"

"It's a long story. Will you come with me while I tell you? I'm going up to Alice's house. James's up there. Dave and I tried to get him to come down here with us, but he wouldn't. He promised that he would come down later, but he never showed up. Dave and I went back up and then Dave sent me to get you. He wants you to hear what James has to say."

"I don't understand, Colby. Why should I go with you up to see James Foster?"

"Because Dave said it was important for you to be there. He knows you have some details that he's lacking and he wants to put the whole story together with James' version. We have to leave right away. Please Ellie, don't make this hard for me. He's waiting for us."

"Colby, this doesn't sound right to me. I want to talk with Dave before I go anywhere with you. Besides, Larry said that no one was to travel the roads tonight. They're too dangerous. Why can't Dave bring James down here?"

"It's too complicated to explain right now, Ellie. You can bring Buddy if that makes you feel any better. The phones aren't working, so we can only talk to Dave on the car radio. Let's get started. You can talk to Dave on the way."

"Colby, I have to admit I don't trust you. This whole story just doesn't make any sense to me. Now maybe that's just because I got knocked dopey, and I'm woozy from the meds, but I'm not going up to Alice's house with you alone. Someone else will have to come if you expect me to go."

"All right. Pauline will go with us. She's bored and looking for something to do."

"I don't know if Pauline's the right person, Colby. Aren't you and she on the outs? I thought you two were fighting."

"Oh no. We fight all the time and then make up and then fight again. That's our pattern. Everything's fine with us now. Come on, Ellie. Dave's waiting for us and we had better go before the roads get any worse."

I tried to move closer to the edge of the bed. I was lightheaded and everything seemed to whirl around.

"Give me a minute, Colby. Get out of the dorm and wait for me in the hall. I'll be out as soon as I can."

Colby slipped out the door into the hallway. I tried to concentrate on what Colby had said, but my head hurt so much it was hard to follow the logic he had proposed for justifying my appearance at Alice's house. Finally, I just gave up thinking. I was too confused to consider anything rationally. I decided to do just as Dave said. I trusted him. And Colby said Dave needed me to listen to something James was saying. I stood up slowly and waited for the vertigo to stop. I leashed Buddy and walked little by little out into the hallway. Colby took my arm and led me to the Inn's front door. Pauline was standing there with her umbrella.

"Wait a minute," I said. "This looks like a set up to me. Why are you here, Pauline?"

"Colby asked me to go for a ride with him. I'm so bored and nervous just sitting here; I thought a wild ride up hill would help distract me from my worries. I'm glad to have you and Buddy along."

"Did Colby tell you we're going up to Alice's house to meet with Dave and James?"

"Right now, Ellie, I don't care where we go, as long as I can get out of that crowd for a while. I'm not really a group kind of person. That's one reason I became a librarian. I like it quiet. So a ride right now is just what I need."

I looked at her. She was smiling and seemed to have forgotten her anger at me completely. I just couldn't figure her out and trying to just made my head hurt more.

"Remember, Colby," I said as he led me outside, holding on to my arm tightly. "I'm not moving an inch until I talk with Dave."

"Right. I'll radio him right away. Just hop in and get settled." He helped me up into the cab of the SUV. The front seat was wide enough for us all. Buddy and I sat in the middle where I could reach the microphone easily. Pauline sat next to the side door. Colby started up the engine.

"What are you doing, Colby? I said I wasn't going anywhere until Dave verifies his request."

"Please stop worrying, Ellie. I have to have the car going to power the radio. I'll contact him right away." He cast a worried look at Pauline as he fiddled with the radio controls. Pauline just stared straight ahead.

The only sound the radio emitted was loud crackly static.

Pauline snapped, "Get on with it, Colby. I don't have all night."

"Seems like the reception is poor. Probably because of all the downed lines and transformers. They would interfere with our transmission. I'll keep trying as we drive up hill, Ellie. The reception is bound to improve."

Colby started the SUV and headed out the Inn's driveway. He continued to turn knobs and dials. Once he pounded on the dashboard as if that would help.

"Well, sorry Ellie. We can't send or receive right now. You'll have to wait until we get there. Don't worry. Everything'll be just fine."

I didn't reply. I didn't think everything would be just fine and I was regretting that I ever got into this vehicle. The further we went the clearer my mind became, whether it was the cold air or the affects of the medication wearing off.

"Stop the truck, Colby. I'm getting out. I'm not going anywhere with you and Pauline. Let's get Herb to go with us. Then I'll go."

Colby kept driving. "Herb's busy. He's with Larry. Don't worry. Everything will be alright, Ellie. Trust me." Colby was anxious and his words tumbled out, serious and strained. He glanced at Pauline again.

Colby started to say "Can't we just…" when Pauline screamed at him. "Just keep going, Colby. Don't think. Drive."

I started to struggle and reach for the door, but Pauline pushed against me and held me back against the seat. I was so dizzy, I couldn't fight her. Buddy growled.

"Tell that dog to shut up or I'll shoot him," Pauline said.

I pulled Buddy close and wrapped my arms around him. He was all I had now.

The Shorter Road wasn't in such bad shape yet, but I could see a lot of destruction along the way. Trees were toppled; culverts were overrun with foaming water. Some culverts were undermined and heaved up to the surface of the road. Newly formed waterways were everywhere, trying to find the most direct route downhill. The new streams were eroding the earth around the tree roots and threatening several driveways. I saw several houses which looked like they were sitting in the middle of a pond.

When we arrived at Alice's house, there were no lights. Of course, I reminded myself, the power is off. Pauline opened the SUV door and pulled me out. Colby held me on one side and Pauline on the other as we walked through the drizzle to the front door. It was open and we walked in. They pushed Buddy outside and closed the door.

Colby yelled, "Hey, we're here. Where're you?"

There was no answer. I called out, "Dave, it's Ellie. I'm here."

A dim light appeared at the end of the front hall. As it came closer I could make out that James Foster was holding the taper. He nodded to us.

"Where's Dave?" I asked, feeling very frightened. What was I doing here?

James answered, "Follow me, right down the hall in the library."

We followed James to Alice's favorite room. Throughout her life Alice had collected the great works of art and art history. The books filled the library shelves from floor to ceiling. Most of the books had been covered with finely worked leather. The candlelight and the light coming from the fire in large stone fireplace that filled one wall of the library revealed their sheen. Even in the dim light I could see that no one else was in the room.

Chapter 30

"WHERE'S DAVE?" I asked, whirling around and facing James, Pauline and Colby who were blocking the only exit. "What's going on? Why did you want me to come all the way up here? What're you up to?"

The trio looked at me. Only Pauline showed any expression on her face.

"Thanks for coming, Ellie. My little scheme to take you out of the action backfired. I didn't mean to hurt you, really. I'm truly sorry about the cuts on your head. I just meant to knock you out until I could hide you in that old wine cellar secret storage hold. I discovered that place back in high school when I was working at the Inn. That hole was just the perfect spot. Hardly anyone knew about it. I just needed to get you to stop your damn investigation. You've been too successful. You've learned some things that you weren't supposed to know. If that dog hadn't interfered and tracked you down, everything would have been taken care of. I would have come back and let you out when the whole thing blew over. Really, I would have. But now we have to do something about you, however unpleasant or distasteful that may be."

"God, Pauline," said Colby. "It was you. I didn't know you were the one who hurt Ellie. What have you done?"

James, Colby and Pauline looked at each other. Pauline said, "We have to figure out how to get out of this mess without anyone else finding out."

"Finding out what? What mess?" I asked.

"Just hold on, Pauline," said James. "I don't want anything to do with this or with whatever you're planning. You told me I had to stay up here and wait for you to come. I did that and that's all I'm going to do. You can't hold Callie over my head anymore. I won't let you. I'm going to tell Dave."

Colby said, "Tell Dave what, James? What did Pauline hold over your head? Did you know she's been threatening me for thirteen years? She said she would ruin my life if I told anyone what happened at the Wilson's that night."

"You were there, too? I don't believe it. You never said anything."

I looked from James to Colby and back again. I was in shock and I think Colby and James were, too. What had happened that night at the Wilson's?

"I couldn't," said Colby. "Pauline said she would tell them I killed the Wilsons if I said anything. Everyone would have believed her before me. You never said anything either. I didn't know you were there either."

Pauline laughed. "Well, now both of you know. Isn't it funny how after all these years, you both have learned something new?"

"There's nothing funny about this, Pauline. It's sick. You're really sick. Just what did happen at the Wilson's? Now I want to hear the whole story from beginning to end," said Colby.

"Me, too," added James.

I was forgotten. I edged slowly toward the door, inch by inch. If I could get enough distance between them and me I might be able to make a break for it. They were so involved with each other; they didn't notice my slight movements. Suddenly, Buddy started to bark outside. All three looked at the door and saw me. I turned and started to run.

Pauline lunged toward me and caught hold of my arm. She threw me down on the floor and pulled a gun from her pocket. She stood behind where I lay, her back to the door, aiming the gun at me and James and Colby.

"Put down the gun, Pauline," said Colby. "You don't need that. Put it down."

Pauline waved the gun in front of Colby.

"Put yours down, pretty boy," she said. "Do it now, or I'll shoot Ellie right through the head."

Colby removed his gun from his holster and laid it on the floor. "Kick it over to me."

Colby complied and Pauline bent down and picked up Colby's gun.

"Now, I have two," she laughed. "I'm ready to tell the story, the whole story to you all. Are you ready to hear it, every juicy bit?"

I nodded. I don't know what Colby and James did, because I couldn't take my eyes off of Pauline. I was terrified that she would shoot me.

"Don't pretend you don't know, Ellie. I know you caught on to the whole thing. Josie and then Sarah probably gave you bits of information and you took it from there. So you guessed that I killed Callie Wilson? I swear I never told a living soul about that. The only ones who could have guessed were Colby and James and I made sure they would never say anything."

"You killed Callie Wilson?" I was amazed.

I looked at Pauline. "Pauline, honestly, I am totally confused. I don't know what you are talking about. If you did kill your friend,

Callie, I didn't know about it. I was never investigating the Wilson murders. What does any of this have to do with me?"

"You would have made the connection soon. You were getting too close to finding out about Alice."

I just let her talk. If she thought I knew who killed Alice, I would just let her think it. She didn't have to know I didn't have a clue yet, only suspects.

"I made Colby bring you here tonight. He didn't want to. He never wants to do anything I ask, but he has to, don't you, Colby? Or they'll find out and you'll end up in prison."

"Pauline, shut up," said Colby. "I have had it. There can't be any more blood spilled. I'm not going to let you do anything to Ellie. I've decided to tell Dave everything. I think he knows me well enough now, to believe me and not you about what happened at the Wilson's."

"I'm with you, Colby," said James. "Pauline has blackmailed me long enough. I'll go with you. Two of us will carry more weight. Pauline, you're going to be caught and you can't do anything about it."

Pauline pointed the gun at them. "Which of you wants to be first? Or, since I have two guns, I could kill you both at the same time. Is that what you want? Now both of you shut up and sit down on the floor where I can keep my eye on you. You aren't going anywhere and aren't telling Dave anything. You wanted to hear the story. Well here it is."

Colby and James sat on the floor and leaned against the wall. For the time being there was little they could do. Pauline had the upper hand.

"I want you all to know I didn't mean to kill Callie. It is very important to me that you understand it was only an accident. I didn't make it happen. I'm not a bad person. I was only sixteen then. I was Callie's best friend. Actually, I was her only friend. Her parents didn't let her do anything, but go to school. They did allow me to go to her house to do homework with her and sometimes they let me stay for the weekend. I felt so sorry for Callie that I hung out with her, even though I would rather have done things with my other friends more often. I was going out with Colby then. Some weekends I would tell my parents that I was staying at the Wilson's and sneak off with Colby and spend the time with him."

Colby said, "That was a long time ago, Pauline. Why are you bringing all this stuff up now? Just get on with it."

"Just hold on, Colby. I want Ellie to understand that I am not an evil person. I didn't mean to kill Callie. You know that. It just happened."

James said, "Pauline, it didn't just happen. It was a terrible mistake. You' were trying to help Callie get out of the house. You didn't think she would slip and fall. It all turned out so badly. I was horrified that Callie was dead, just lying there on the ground, with her head all bloody. Even after all these years, I can't forget it, can't get the pictures out of my mind. That's one reason why I've stayed away for so long."

"Well, you should've just stayed away forever, for all I care," Pauline said. "If you hadn't come back, maybe none of this would have had to happen."

"Don't blame that on me," yelled James. "It was Alice who asked me to come back. She said if I didn't come she would tell everything to Dave."

"Stop it. Stop it now. Fighting about the past won't help us now. Let's just get on with it, Pauline," said Colby.

"I am telling my story the way I want to," said Pauline. "No more interruptions, please. So, Ellie, as I was saying, I'm telling you this so you will understand that I'm not to blame. It was all Colby's fault really. James was Callie's boyfriend, but he could only see her at school. James wanted to go to her parents and explain about wanting to date Callie, but Callie said not to. She was afraid of her parents. Then Colby started to flirt with Callie at school and I think she liked him better than James, but Colby was my boyfriend. What a bitch she was. Callie wasn't content having one guy; she wanted them both. I wanted to kill her. Now, don't take me literally. I didn't really want to kill her. That's just an expression. Right? I did want to punish Callie though. Colby was my boyfriend. She already had James. So, I decided to try to get her into trouble. I wanted to get back at Colby and James, too, for choosing Callie over me."

Silence fell in the dim room. I stood there absolutely confused and terrified. James and Colby leaned against the wall, staring at Pauline. I wondered what was going to happen next.

Pauline started talking again. "I was invited to her house for the weekend. I told my parents that I was going out with Colby and didn't mention that I was going to the Wilson's. When I got to Callie's house, I told Callie that Colby and I had broken up and were just best friends now and that he said he wanted to come over to see her after it was dark and her parents were asleep. She got so excited that I almost got sick. I told her I would cover for her with her parents if they discovered she was gone. Of course, Colby wasn't really coming. I just made that part up."

Pauline was really enjoying telling her story. Her eyes were flashing in the candlelight and bright spots of red had colored her cheeks. She was performing, I realized, and we were her audience.

"When it was dark and her parents had gone to bed, I helped Callie to escape from her second story window. We tied a sheet together and lowered it out and tied the other end to her radiator. Then she climbed out. But something went wrong. She slipped and I tried to grab her but I couldn't hold on and she fell to the ground. I was so scared. I ran down stairs and around the house to where she was laying. She had hit her head on a rock and she was dead. I didn't know what to do. I left her there and went into the house and called James. He came over in his parents' car. He wanted to call Dave, but that would have ruined everything. I was afraid people would blame me. I convinced him that we should just say that Callie ran away from home. That way I wouldn't get into any trouble. It wasn't really my fault, but I was afraid people would think it was and then all my plans to escape this town, to go to college and start a new life would be destroyed. So we put Callie's body in the trunk of the car."

"I didn't want any part of it," James said. "Pauline was crazy. She said if I didn't help her get rid of Callie's body that she'd tell everyone that I killed Callie. She was going to say that I had come to take Callie away. After all, everyone knew Callie and I were going steady and that we could never see each other outside of school. But, Pauline threatened to say that Callie didn't want to go with me because she liked Colby now and so I killed her. I would never kill Callie. I loved her. But I was afraid that Pauline would be more believable than me. So I went along with her. I wish I never had. It changed my whole life. Ruined it. Destroyed my relationship with my family."

"Oh come on, James. You haven't had it so hard. All you had to do was take the body and hide it. You did a good job of that, at least. We might have gotten away with our story that Callie probably killed her parents and ran away, if only her skull didn't turn up."

"But Callie didn't kill her parents, Pauline. You did," said Colby. "And that's how I got mixed up in the whole mess."

"I had to, you know that by now. I didn't want to. But they heard James drive off and started to come downstairs. They would have known that something wasn't right. I grabbed Mr. Wilson's rifle from the gun case. I didn't even know it was loaded. I made Mrs. Wilson find some duct tape and tape up Mr. Wilson. Then I hit Mrs. Wilson over the head with the gun and taped her up. Then I didn't know what to do. Mr. Wilson said he would get me, no matter how long it took and I just went blank. I don't remember very much after that. I must have blacked out or something. The next thing I knew, the Wilsons were all bloody and dead. There was blood on them and all over the floor. I thought someone had come in and killed them and that I must have fainted."

"That's not what you told me when you called, Pauline," said Colby. "You said something bad happened and you needed me to come over to the Wilson's right away."

"So? If I had told you they were dead, you wouldn't have come. You would have gone to Dave and that was the last thing I wanted."

Colby looked at me. "When I got there she told me that Callie had flown into a fit and killed her parents and run away. Pauline was afraid that she might be suspected of being the murderer or an accomplice because she was there. She didn't have any blood on her that I could see, even though the floors and ceilings and walls were totally blood spattered. So I believed her. I thought Callie had flipped out or something. I never suspected Pauline at all. Now I know that high velocity rifles are so powerful that most of the blood goes up and back, leaving only a mist of blood about three or four feet around the victim. All a shooter has to do is stay beyond that range and she will be virtually clean of any blood. But I didn't know that back then. Pauline asked me to clean up the house and get rid of any evidence that might show she had been there that night. She said if I didn't help her, she would tell everyone that I had come to take Callie out and her parents got furious with me and so I killed them and then killed Callie when she wouldn't go with me and hid her body. She said everyone knew I had a bad history and it was her word against mine. I couldn't win that battle, I knew. So, I took all of Pauline's things out and wiped the gun off as best I could. I put Pauline in the car and took her home. We were each other's alibis. We said we were together that night and her parents verified it and of course, everyone believed us. Why would anyone think we had anything to do with the murders?"

"So, you held both James and Colby hostage?" I asked Pauline.

"Yes, and it worked because neither one knew about the part the other had played. I had both of them scared. And there were no clues for Dave to work with. After a few months the case went cold. Just a skull and that was it. I never figured out how the skull was found because I never knew what James did with Callie's body. I didn't want to know."

"I put her in a big pile of brush and branches that the loggers had left way up that logging road to Diamond Mountain, up by Mike's place. Animals must have got to her and scattered her bones. Somehow the skull got near the bank of the Alder Creek and that's where Dave found it on one of his search missions. I can't bear to think about it. I had nightmares for years. I left town right after I graduated from high school that year. I couldn't stand it any longer. I told my parents that I was gambling, but that wasn't true. I stole from them for two reasons. One, to pay Pauline to keep her mouth shut. She was saving money for college and blackmailed me. The ten thousand dollars wasn't to pay off a gambling debt. It was to pay off Pauline. I never saw my father or mother again. I had shamed them and myself. They believed I was a liar, a thief and a no good gambler. They died never knowing the truth."

I was surprised by how sorry for James and Colby I felt. What a tragedy. Two young teens pulled into an impossible situation by a psychopathic friend. How hard it must have been for them to live knowing what they did.

"Weren't you afraid?" I asked them all.

"I knew Pauline was going off to school and I would probably never see her again. So I kept telling myself I only had to wait until she was gone and then I could put it all behind me. I didn't know she would return to Hummingbird Falls," said Colby.

"But I came back to marry you, Colby," said Pauline with a sneer. "Only you kept putting me off. I tried to help you find your mother, hoping you would like me better."

"How could you even think I could stand you, Pauline? I saw you standing next to a room filled with blood and two dead bodies. You threatened me. I hated you. I still do. You give me the creeps. I will never have anything to do with you. I have told you that."

"Too bad you did. Because a lot of people had to suffer for that, Colby. Alice, Josie, Sarah and now Ellie. All because you have a weak stomach."

"What are you saying, Pauline? Did you kill Alice and Josie? Did you hurt Sarah?" asked Colby.

"Yes. I did. I didn't mean to kill Alice, but I did. She was chasing after me with a rod iron stick. I backed the car into her by accident. Then when she was trying to get up, all hurt and bloody, I put her out of her misery. I hit her with the iron stick. Josie had to die because she saw me. She was standing in the road. I went after her with the stick, but she disappeared. I had to sneak up to her house right after the town meeting and Ellie and Sarah almost caught me. Sarah was an accident, too. She slipped when I pushed her and she hit her head and went down. I put the opened envelope in her hand. I wrote that note to put the attention on Colby. Ellie had to be put out of the way because she was beginning to suspect something. I had to do it, Colby. I had to do it all? Don't you see? It had to be done or they would find out."

A loud noise interrupted Pauline. Flashlights flickered down the hall. Men's voices were calling. "Police. Stay where you are. Put your hands in back of your head and lie down on the floor. Now. Do it now."

Chapter 31

AS DAVE, MIKE, Herb and several other deputized men surged down the hall toward the library, Colby, James and I hit the floor with our hands behind our heads. I didn't want to take the chance that in the dim light they would mistake me for someone else, or think I had a weapon.

Pauline ran for the library French doors that opened onto the circular porch. She pushed them open and disappeared outside just as Dave reached the library and shone his flashlight around.

I yelled, "Dave, it's Pauline. She just ran out the door. She did it. She did it all."

Dave flashed his light on me. "Ellie, get up. What did you say? Pauline? Where is she?"

Colby answered. "She just ran out the door. She has two guns, so watch yourself."

Colby and James got to their feet and started toward the French doors.

Dave said, "Hold it a minute, fellas. I need to know what's going on here. Why does Pauline have two guns and what're you doing here?"

"There's no time to explain everything now, Dave," said Colby. "One of the guns is mine. She's getting away."

Just then we heard tires spinning in the gravel driveway.

"Damn, I left my truck running with the keys in it," said Mike as he ran for the door. "She's stolen my truck."

Dave and the others ran outside. The tail lights of Mike's car were disappearing down the driveway. Dave and Mike jumped into the patrol SUV. Dave flicked on the flashing lights and siren and took off after her. Colby, James, Buddy and I stuffed ourselves into the passenger seat and back cab of Herb's four-wheel drive truck. The other trucks followed after us.

"What's this all about?" asked Herb as he skillfully steered his huge vehicle around the curves of the driveway. We could see Dave's lights ahead, but Pauline had disappeared into the dark rainy night.

"Just concentrate on your driving, Herb," Colby said. "You'll find out everything very soon, I'm sure."

We raced down the Shorter Road, avoiding the worst potholes, and trying to stay centered on the road so the badly eroded soft shoulders couldn't grab at the tires. Dave's SUV was swinging all over the road ahead, fishtailing and bumping into the air after hitting fallen branches or bunched up asphalt. He was moving so fast that we often lost sight of him on the curves.

We hurtled around one curve and Herb braked sharply and skidded sideways as he tried to avoid hitting Dave's SUV which was stopped in the middle of the road. We all jumped out and ran to the Police vehicle. The headlights revealed skid marks on the road, crushed bushes and a downed tree. Just beyond the tree, Mike's truck was hanging over the edge of a ravine that dropped fifty feet down to a creek that was roaring its way down to join the Coldwater River.

We made our way to Mike's truck. The front driver's door had been ripped off by the tree. There was no one in the truck. Pauline was gone.

"Oh no," I screamed.

"Search in a circle as far as you can around the truck. She has to be somewhere near here. Walk carefully; look for tracks, broken branches, anything that might indicate where she is headed. She is probably hurt pretty badly, so she won't be far off."

Dave called to the group gathered around. "Ellie, you and James go sit in Herb's truck and lock the doors. Drive slowly on down to the Inn and wait there for me. Keep your mouths shut. Don't tell anyone what has gone on up here. I don't want anyone else getting enraged and trying to take the law into their own hands. Colby, you come with me."

The men spread out, shining their flashlights along the ground. I could see the rain falling as the lights skipped here and there. As they moved further into the woods and out from the road, an eerie scene emerged. Dark shapes of the men were etched against dark trees, holding little beams of light that flickered and disappeared and reappeared as they walked through the thick forest. I shivered and was glad to turn and walk with James to Herb's truck. We climbed in and I hugged Buddy as James boosted the heat. We watched from our perch as the search continued and then drove down to the Inn.

Chapter 32

IT SEEMED LIKE hours passed before the men returned to the Inn.

"Didn't find a thing," Dave said. "She just disappeared. We can't see anything out there and the rain's wiping out any signs she might have made. We stopped back to gather more men to search."

"Did we lose the bridge? Is the town flooded?" asked a food table lady.

"Not to my knowledge," said Dave. "Has anyone seen Pauline? We have been looking for her."

No one spoke. Everyone looked confused. They had no idea of what had happened and what was going on.

"Relax folks," said Dave. "Larry should be by with a weather update pretty soon. Until then, how about finding us some dry clothes and some hot coffee?"

People seemed relieved to be given something to do. In no time, hot coffee and dry clothes were available. The search group had been assembled and received instructions on where to look for Pauline.

"We will leave again to resume the search just as soon as I find out from you three what happened up at Alice's," Dave said. "I have Mike's bloodhounds on the way. They are pretty good even when it's wet. Human scent sticks even in the rain, although it is tougher on the dogs to follow it. But Mike's dogs are the best in the county and at least have a chance of tracking Pauline. Now, let's start with you, Ellie."

I told him all the details of the last hours I had spent. As I recounted the events, I realized how close I had come to being killed, not once, but twice. I was exhausted when I finished my story and looked at Dave with weary eyes. James went next, expanding his tale into the past. He went into more detail about what had happened at the Wilson's that night. He finished with tears in his eyes.

"Alice asked me to come back here to talk with her. I thought it was about the estate, but she said Pauline had told her that I had murdered the Wilson's and that she was going to tell Dave if Alice didn't give her enough money to go to grad school. Alice found me somehow and called. I had never left a forwarding address with anyone because I didn't want Pauline to find me. Alice told me she wanted me to come home; it was a matter of life and death. When I got here, she begged me to turn myself in. I told her I was innocent and had been blackmailed by Pauline as well. We argued over and over about what to do. She wanted me to make a clean slate of it. She wanted me to turn myself in. I was dubious. I didn't think anyone would believe me. The very night that Alice died, I'd finally agreed that I'd go in to talk with you, Dave. Alice said she had some people to meet with that night, but she'd go with me in the morning to see you. She promised to support me. That meant a lot to me, after all these years. I took a couple of sleeping pills, and, of course, Alice and I'd been drinking quite a lot. I feel into a deep sleep and didn't wake up until morning. She wasn't there, so I was waiting for her to return before I talked to you. She never came back." James sobbed softly into his hands.

"Now you, Colby," Dave said. Colby started talking, marking events chronologically from when Pauline, James and he were all in high school together. Dave watched him closely, nodding now and then, shaking his head in disbelief at other times. When Colby finished telling his story, Dave looked grim.

"So, your story is that you never touched any of the Wilson's?" Dave asked Colby.

"No, I swear. I haven't hurt or killed anyone. Pauline told me Callie killed her parents and ran away, but it was Pauline who killed the Wilson's. It had to be. And she killed Alice and Josie as well. She tried to kill Sarah and Ellie, too."

"I can buy she killed the Wilson's. That story makes sense and you and James are both saying the same things. But what about Alice? Why would Pauline kill Alice?"

Colby looked up at Dave and then around at the rest of us. "I think I can tell you why. Pauline must have learned from Alice that night that I had told her the whole story and that I was going to tell you everything the next day. Alice told her that James was admitting his part, too. Pauline had to stop that from happening. So she killed Alice."

"When, how?" Dave asked.

"Sometime after I left her house that night," said Colby. "James was asleep upstairs. Alice had called me and asked me to come to talk with her. She said it was important. When I got there she was a little drunk, but she told me James had confessed his part in hiding Callie's body and suspected that I had some part in that event as well. I wasn't going to say anything, but when your mother looks at you and begs you to tell, it is hard to resist."

"Your mother?" Dave asked in unison with James and me.

"Yes," Colby said. "Alice was my mother. I wanted so badly to find my birth mother and to learn who my father was. It became an obsession with me and Pauline agreed to help me. I think she thought she would be indispensable to me if she helped and that I would be so grateful I would marry her. But I hated Pauline. I have hated her ever since the night of the Wilson's murder. She makes me sick. Anyway, she used the library computer programs to trace my initial adoption and got in contact with the agency. She found out that Alice Foster had given me up for adoption shortly after my birth. Pauline tried to convince me to blackmail Alice for a lot of money. She said the Foster family money was rightfully mine and I should go after it. It would serve Alice right."

"I finally confronted Alice a while back. She was overwhelmed. At first, she didn't believe it. Then she checked it out for herself. Then, she couldn't stop crying, she was so happy to find me. I was delighted myself. I have always liked and respected Alice. Then I find out she is my mother and loves me too. Wow. It was just like a movie with a good ending. We started to spend a lot of time together. I think people thought I was visiting her for romantic reasons and I just let them think that. Alice and I had decided to keep the secret for a while longer."

"That is what we all thought. We knew there was quite an age difference, but you made a handsome couple. And everyone thinks you are irresistible, Colby. Some thought you were after her money. Others thought Alice was just so lonely she reached out for you. Now, I understand. Actually, there is quite a resemblance between the two of you. What about your father?" asked Dave.

"Alice told me she was engaged to a man she loved very much. She got pregnant and her fiancé got scared and ran off. She has never seen him since. I do plan to look for him now that I know who he is. She went to Europe so no one would know she was having a baby and just before the birth came back to the U.S. She gave birth at a home for unwed mothers not too far from here. She never saw me. The social worker took me away to a family who wanted a baby boy. In those days the birth mother wasn't allowed to know anything about the adoptive family and although she tried to find me through the years, she couldn't get anywhere. She went on with her life. And I went on with mine."

"Alice asked me to keep her secret for a little while longer. She and I were just starting to build a relationship when she was killed." Tears leaked out of Colby's eyes and trickled down his cheeks. He looked just like a lost little boy, wanting and missing his mother.

"So, you told her about the Wilson's?" Dave asked softly.

"Yes," said Colby. "The night that she died. She already knew James' part and had been told by Pauline that I was the killer. She wanted to know if I had anything to do with it. I told her everything. She said she would call Pauline and give her a chance to turn herself in before we went to Dave to tell him our stories. That way it wouldn't go so hard for Pauline. Alice had always thought of Pauline as a nice hard working girl. She felt compassion for her and decided to try to help her, rather than turn her in. That turned out to be a mistake."

"I met Pauline on the road before I met with Alice that night. I think she waited until I left and then went in and threatened Alice. Pauline said that Alice chased her with an iron pole, but I don't think I believe that, knowing Alice and Pauline as I do now. More likely, Pauline decided she needed to get rid of Alice, otherwise Alice, James and I were going to Dave. So, Pauline killed her and then took her down to the falls and dumped her in. Josie must have seen her. I don't know how she thought she would get away with it. But I guess she almost did. I guess after Josie, Sarah and Ellie, James and I were next on her list."

Colby shuddered. "She was going to kill us, Dave. After she let us know how clever she had been, she was going to shoot the three of us. I have to admit, I was really scared."

Dave slowly shook his head, stunned by all he had heard.

"Thanks for telling me the truth, James and Colby. I knew something wasn't right about Pauline, but I just couldn't put my finger on it. On the outside she was the perfect librarian, efficient, rather compliant, and always helpful. She was one of us. I guess there was a whole lot more going on inside. Well, I will need to talk to both of you later. Meanwhile, I would like you both to sit right here and write down your statements in full detail. Start at the beginning and don't leave anything out. I'm going to continue the search for Pauline. She is out there somewhere and I will find her. You can count on that. She isn't going to get away again."

Dave rose with determination and headed for the front lobby of the Inn. I watched him gather a large group of men together and give them directions from the map he held in his hands. The search party was outfitted in rain gear, mountain hiking boots, backpacks, walkie-talkies, and large flashlights. In addition, each man was given a gun and warned not to use it unless absolutely necessary. Pauline was to be taken alive, if at all possible. But they were warned that she was armed and very dangerous.

"Don't take any chances," Dave said as the men started out the door. "Be safe out there."

I made my way over to Dave. "What about me, Dave? Do you want my statement, too?"

Dave smiled down at me. "It's been quite a day for you, hasn't it Ellie? Yes, of course, I want your statement, too. Then, I want you to lie down and rest. Your head must be aching terribly."

"It is. But to be truthful, I haven't really had time to notice it until now. I'll write out my statement and then rest. But there is one more thing."

"Yes, Ellie. What is it?" Dave asked.

"Do you think we have a good enough case against Pauline? No one actually saw any of the murders, or attacks, except Josie and she is dead. We only have Colby and James to testify to what they saw after the Wilsons were already dead. I can testify that I heard Pauline confess to the murders tonight, but isn't that hearsay and can't she just deny it? There isn't any evidence to convict her."

Dave said, "We will get a confession. I guarantee that. Sounds like Pauline is spilling all that she has done and maybe she is having some kind of emotional break down and will be relieved to tell us everything that she has been keeping stored up for thirteen years. And we will find the rod iron that killed Alice and Josie, too. While we might not be able to try her for first-degree murder for the Wilsons or Alice, we can get her for Josie's premeditated murder. Don't worry, Ellie. She will be in jail for a long time."

Dave left and I took Buddy and myself to my cot in the corner of the women's dorm and fell asleep while writing out my statement.

Chapter 33

I WOKE WITH the light of a full moon blasting down into my face. I sat straight up and stared out the dining room window. I never saw such a beautiful sight. The moon was riding high and was surrounded by sprinkles of stars. Thin wisps of clouds were scurrying east. It had stopped raining.

Buddy and I jumped out of the cot. All around me, women were waking up and laughing with joy. Outside the room I could hear other people shouting and clapping. We all rushed out to the lobby and then down onto the drive in front of the Inn on the Hill. We danced and sang. Some sunk to their knees in prayer. The rain had stopped.

Larry pulled up in the Hummingbird Falls' maintenance truck. He got out and stretched his arms over his head.

"Hallelujah," he yelled. "The rain stopped."

The crowd quieted to hear what he had to say.

"I think we are going to make it." Larry called out. "The river will crest in a few hours, but I think it will be low enough to save the bridge and the town."

Great cheers went up to the starry skies. People hugged on another and cried.

Larry yelled, "Folks, the bad news is you have to stay the rest of tonight at the Inn. I have to be sure that you will be safe before you can go back to your homes. If it is not raining tomorrow, those of you in the valley can head for home. You will probably need help pumping your basements and fixing any appliances that were in the cellar. Dump any stuff that is ruined out front and the road crew will come by in the next weeks to pick it up, or in a day or two you can take it to the dump yourselves. Keep a list for the insurance companies and FEMA who will be involved as soon as they can get here. Any downed trees, call me and leave a message. Any downed lines call the North Star utilities people. Watch for gas lines. Any worries call the gas company and let me know too. All power should be on in town in a few days at the latest. It might even be on now in some areas. I know town hall, the Little Church and the Inn by Bridge just got their power back and there are some phone lines up and running, too. I'll go over all this again tomorrow morning."

"Now you folks living up in the hills will have to stay down here longer than you probably want to. Power won't be on up there for a while. Trucks can't get up the roads to fix the wires and transformers until the roads are fixed. We have heavy equipment coming from all over to help us out, so just sit tight until I give you the word you can return home."

A mixture of cheers and complaints followed Larry's announcement, depending upon whether the individual lived up hill or in town. I guessed I wouldn't see my cottage for quite a while and wondered if the bear would come back to finish his dinner that was coagulating into a hardened mess on my kitchen floor.

"What about Alice's memorial service?" I asked.

"Well, the Little Church is dry. The water came up to the door, but never moved high enough to get inside that structure or the library. The Inn across the street just got its power back on. So, since everyone who would be attending the service is here all ready, I'd say, let's go ahead with the service and the reception tomorrow. If we don't have everything you originally planned for, well, what does that really matter? We certainly all understand. More important to honor Alice and we can use the service to give thanks that the rain has stopped as well."

I turned to the crowd. "Just come as you are tomorrow. Alice would be the first one to say it doesn't matter about the dress or fixings, just the community gathering together for her would make her smile."

Everyone nodded. We headed back inside to get what sleep we could before the sun rose. The blessed sun. There was a feeling of spirit and thankfulness that stirred me and reminded me once again how much I loved this world, this town and the people in it.

I worried about Dave and the searchers as I lay back down on my cot. I hoped that they would find Pauline soon and bring her back to face justice. I wanted them to be able to celebrate Alice's life and the survival of Hummingbird Falls with their families, neighbors and friends.

I fell asleep thinking about the forget-me-nots that I had planned to bring to Alice's memorial service, sorry that I hadn't been able to gather them to put in a vase next to her picture on the altar.

Mid June, shortly after solstice, I noticed flecks of brilliant blue floating about nine inches above the soil in the back garden, up by the shed. When I bent down to investigate I saw tiny blue flowers in little curled sprays attached to two uncoiling branches growing from slightly hairy stalks. The wind danced them lightly and the blue seemed to float in the air like little pieces of sky. The sun yellow centers held the five blue petals, the sunny summer sky remembered in the bloom of the flower. The Forget-me-nots had arrived.

In the language of flowers, Forget-me-nots are symbolic of love and constancy. There is a lovely Persian legend, told by the poet Shiraz, that illustrates the love and affection that endears the flower to us all.

"It was in the golden morning of the early world, when an angel sat weeping outside the closed gates of Eden. He had fallen from his high estate through loving a daughter of earth, nor was he permitted to enter again until she whom he loved had planted the flowers of the Forget-me-not in every corner of the world. He returned to earth, and assisted her, and they went hand in hand over the world, planting the Forget-me-nots. When their task was ended they entered Paradise together; for the fair woman, without tasting the bitterness of death, became immortal like the angel, whose love her beauty had won, when she sat by the river twining the Forget-me-nots in her hair."

There is something about Forget-me-nots that grabs me. There is the beauty, of course, the fragile floating of blue, too soon gone like the summer skies in the mountain regions.. The fact that their flowering time is so fleeting makes them more precious. And the sentiment of the various legends about the origin of their name is entrancing. But it is the name of these little flowers that makes me love them as well. Forget-me-not. A wish for remembrance. When the Forget-me-nots complete their short blooming time, not much of the plants are left to demand attention or adoration. Does their name help the gardener to keep them in mind until next year when they return? Is it a plea not to rip out and discard their simple defoliated stalks and plant bright replacements to fill that empty space? Do they need a name that reminds us that they will come back, faithful perennials?

Do not forget. The quiet command is threatening. What if I do forget? What then? Why this demand from a modest mild blue flower?

There are many things I do want to forget: The pain of loss, the sadness of despair, the anger of clashing communications, the trouble in my children's lives, the disruption of our beautiful earth, the intentioned destruction of any sentient being, the unhappiness of anyone I know and love, the deaths of Alice and Josie and of poor Callie Wilson and her parents, who I never even knew. But if I forget? If I forget then I experience greater loss: the moment, the person, the world, and the flower become invisible to me. If I replace them with something new and forget the old, then I have destroyed a part of who I am and what I have experienced.

The plea Forget-me-not asks us to remain present to all from which we part. Forget-me-not because you mean so much to me. Please keep me alive and with you in memory, dreams and love. Forget not that the winter sky will be followed by the spring, that the empty garden will fill again, that the lover will return in memory and dreams. Forget not that the world renews itself through Pella's birthing of new ground, from cone seeds of rotting pine and sprigs of new growth that force themselves into the world through cracks in city sidewalks.

My love for the tender Forget-me-nots is renewed each spring when they return, reflecting the sky, and returning my trust, forging my faith and helping me to remember all that is meaningful to me.

Longfellow considered the forget-me-nots when he looked into the night skies and saw the stars. In *Evangeline* he says:

"Silently, one by one, in the infinite meadows of heaven,

Blossom the lovely stars, the forget-me-nots of the angels."

I slept with sweet dreams of moons and forget-me-nots, and cheering friends.

Chapter 34

IN THE MORNING and under a brilliant blue sky and dazzling sun, we started down to the Little Church, a parade of Hummingbird Falls' folks, ragtag and disheveled, but together. Someone started to sing Amazing Grace and before long we all joined as we walked down the wet road into town to honor one of our best. When we arrived at the Little Church, Dave and the search team were waiting for us. The hounds had followed Pauline's trail and found her with a sprained ankle, cowering under some bushes. She was pretty beat up from the car accident and from bushwhacking through the thick forest. She had lost both guns and was ready to give up. She surrendered gladly, claiming that she was innocent and wanted a lawyer. Dave drove her to the County Jail Infirmary where she was arrested and her injuries were cared for. She would remain there until the bond hearing. Dave and the other men, dirty clothes, muddy boots and all, joined us in celebrating Alice's life.

Afterwards, everyone crossed the street to the Inn for the reception. Fortunately for us, the Inn had a great deal of food available, due to cancellations. They donated the food as well as their full facilities for the memorial reception. They even offered to put up the people who couldn't return to their homes for free, since no tourists would be coming to Hummingbird Falls until all road repairs were finished.

Their phones were now working. I went to a pay phone and called Sandy. He answered with a cheery voice.

"How are things going, Sandy?" I asked.

"Oh Mom, I'm glad you called. Things are going great. I mean it; Marilyn and I are doing really well. We went ahead and have had two sessions already with the couples counselor and we both feel like a lot of the pressure is relieved. It will take a while, though. We have a long way to go, but at least we are starting. By the way, thanks for the advice and Marilyn tried to call you to talk with you, but they said the lines were down up your way. What's going on?'

"Oh nothing, dear. We just had a lot of rain and some lines went down, but the sun is shining now. I am so happy for you both. Keep it up. I can't talk long right now, since I'm on the pay phone, but I'll call you later. Love you."

I disconnected and then called Allison. "Where have you been mom? I have been calling you for days. Forget the loan. Everything has worked out better than I could ever have imagined. If I hadn't left that old job, I would never have been hired by the top research company in the area. Not only did I get a promotion, I am earning more money, too. So everything has worked out fine. I hope I didn't worry you too much."

"No, honey. I knew you would bounce back on top, just like always. Well, I am really busy right now. I'll have to call you later for all the details. Right now it is enough to know you are all right and well."

"Better than that, Mom. Maybe I'll even get a weekend free and come up there for a rest and some peace after all the stress I have been through. A little calm quiet in Hummingbird Falls where nothing ever happens is just what I need."

"Sure, Allison, you know you always have a place here anytime you want. I'll talk to you soon. Love you."

I smiled as I put down the phone. The kids were OK again.

After a very short snack of food, I noticed Mr. Compton arrive. I walked over to him and welcomed him and offered to get him some food, but he wanted to get his business taken care of and get on his way.

"It was hell getting here. I almost turned around. The roads are awful and wires down everywhere. But I made it through. Now, let's just get this done. Are all the beneficiaries here?"

"All that are alive and healthy and free to come," I replied. "Certainly, those in jail or the hospital can't be blamed for not attending."

"Well, I guess we can get around that stipulation, as long as no one refused to come," he answered.

I clinked a spoon against a glass and silenced the crowd. "The following people need to meet in Conference Room A immediately." I read the list of beneficiaries from the list Mr. Compton handed me. The room buzzed with voices after I finished.

Dave and Mary, Colby, Margaret, Mike, James and the Wilsons followed Mr. Compton and me into the conference room. After we all found chairs Mr. Compton began to read the will. When he got to the bequests he slowed down and read very clearly Alice's wishes.

The first several beneficiaries were the charities Alice had designated. She had made some very insightful and caring comments about the work these organizations were doing as well, reminding us all that what we gave to others would become gifts to ourselves in the long run.

Then Mr. Compton continued the reading of bequests to individuals. He started with the bequest to me. Everyone smiled and seemed happy that I would become a Hummingbird Falls full time resident. Then he went on.

"I planned to leave $100,000, to Pauline Hayes, which was to be used exclusively to pay off all her debts and the remainder used to finance a library science graduate program. If she successfully completed the graduate program, she would have received an additional $100,000 to do with as she wished."

A gasp went around the room. Mr. Compton cleared his throat and continued.

"Instead, I leave Pauline one dollar. She can do with it what she wants."

Mr. Compton said, "This was a late change in Alice's will. And this particular bequest will be delayed until the investigation of Alice's homicide is completed. As you may know, perpetrators of murder may not benefit financially from their crime, even if it is only one dollar."

The room applauded and then quieted again.

"To my brother James Foster, I leave the Foster home, a trust fund to manage the property, three acres surrounding the home, as noted in the attached surveyor's map, and all its furnishings, to live in until his death or until he wishes to leave. In the event he does not reside in the home, the property shall pass to the town of Hummingbird Falls with a yearly maintenance account to pay for all upkeep and repair. It is my desire that the home and property be used as a residential home to help foster children. An endowment of $2,000,000 to this end has been placed under the legal guardianship of Mr. Compton, my lawyer, and the Greenberg Federal Bank. I want you to know, James, that I love you and that I am so sorry for all the pain that you have suffered."

Everyone looked at James who had tears streaming down his cheeks.

"I will not disclose the contents of the letter that Alice left for James. It is quite lengthy and is very personal. I will hand it over to James at the end of the reading.

"To my friend Margaret, owner of the Hummingbird Falls Gallery. I leave you my love and a plea that you reconsider your opinions about the future of Hummingbird Falls. In addition, you are to sell all the art work listed below. You will receive the commission of 20% for all you sell. The remainder of 80% will be donated to the foundation to keep Hummingbird Falls free of commercial corporate investments and speculations. I hope you do well with the sales, both for yourself and the community."

Margaret looked shocked. Alice's art work was worth millions. How clever of Alice to position Margaret to benefit from supporting a philosophy she had opposed.

"To Dave and Mary Shaffer, I leave $100,000 in gratitude for their good works for Hummingbird Falls and for their long and faithful friendship. I have been fortunate to have them in my life."

"To Albert Wilson I leave the sum of $500,000. No amount of money could ever replace your family. It is my desire that $250,000 be set aside as a scholarship trust fund in the name of Callie Wilson and that each year a senior from Regional High School will be awarded a grant to use as tuition to a college of his or her choice. The remaining $250,000 is for the Wilson family to use as they see fit."

"To Sarah, loyal and hardworking friend of Hummingbird Falls, I allocate $100,000 for her use as she sees fit. I hope you will use it for a trip around the world Sarah. You deserve it."

"To Mike Greeley I leave a trust fund to cover all his personal and property expenses within reason, with his agreement to cease the sale of any lands remaining on the Greeley Farm and to continue the use and management of the farm lands in good order. Thanks Mike, for working so hard to keep the fields beautiful, even though it has meant hardship for you."

"And finally, to my son, Colby Conners, I leave $2,000,000 to be used as he sees fit. My greatest sadness was giving him up and my greatest joy is finding him again. I hope you know, Colby, that I have always loved you and searched for you. I thank you for accepting me and letting me come back into your life."

Mr. Compton raised his head and surveyed the group. "That's it except for the various charities. I have letters for each of you that Alice asked me to distribute at the close of the reading. If you have any questions, call my office or contact Ellie Hastings who is the executrix of the will. Barring any unforeseen complications, this will can be through probate in about a year, less if all goes well. But, if we run in unforeseen problems, such as someone contesting the will, the settlement could be years away. Thank you for coming."

We all sat in silence, not wanting to stir. The spirit of Alice hung over us and wrapped around us. Finally, Dave stood and said, "I have to move along. I have a lot of paper work to complete. Thank you all. We have been very lucky to know a fine woman like Alice Foster." Mr. Compton handed him his letter from Alice and he and Mary said goodbye and left.

The rest of us stood and gathered our things, received our letters and hugged each other and then made our exits. I stayed behind to make an appointment with Mr. Compton to start the probate proceedings. Then I accompanied him to the front lobby and said goodbye to him.

I registered for a room for the night and found Buddy who had stayed with Jennie while the will was read. I wanted to take a walk, be outside, alone for a while and think about my friend Alice and poor Josie. Before I left the reception, I clinked a glass again and announced that Josie's service would be in the little church tomorrow morning at 10:30 and hoped that everyone would be able to attend. Then I turned and walked out into the sunshine with Buddy by my side.

Printed in the United States
140292LV00004B/55/P

9 780976 810810